BLUE CLOUD

JESSICA HECKET

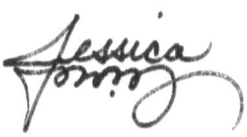

ISBN-13: 978-0-9994364-1-7

1 2 3 4 5 6 7 8 9 10

NKJV
Scripture taken from the New King James Version®.
Copyright © 1982 by Thomas Nelson.
Used by permission. All rights reserved.

Cover Photos by Leslie Connly
Layout/Design & Formatting by Rachael Ritchey

FOR OUT OF MUCH AFFLICTION AND ANGUISH
OF HEART I WROTE TO YOU, WITH MANY TEARS,
NOT THAT YOU SHOULD BE GRIEVED,
BUT THAT YOU MIGHT KNOW THE LOVE WHICH
I HAVE SO ABUNDANTLY FOR YOU.

~ II CORINTHIANS 2:4

*Dream sequences are italicized for the reader's benefit.

"*I sleep, but my heart wakes,*
it is the voice of my beloved knocking . . ." (a)

PART I

I saw a dream which made me afraid,
and the thoughts upon my bed
and the visions of my head troubled me. (b)

In another land,
from another place
How can it be?
That I should see your face?

John Bates looked like a well-worn Englishman. His walk still carried the dignity of a gentleman, yet his apparel had lost most of its formal perfection. It was not his rumpled clothing, however, that made him stand out in the crowd along the docks. His piercing blue eyes and fair skin were a rare sight in Africa. Around him women carried baskets on their heads, and men gazed at him disinterestedly. The sandy earth ran right up to the sea as if unaware of the streets and buildings resting upon it. The place was filled with colorful garbs of local people. Every few minutes John would catch the friendly smile of someone whom he had met in his time here. One such friendly face rushed into his legs with exuberance that nearly knocked him over. "Mr. John, Mr. John!" A little girl named Becca hugged his legs affectionately. Looking up into his face she asked with sad conviction, "You are really leaving?" He gently set his bag down and kneeling beside the child he took her upon his knee. "I'm afraid so. Now, where is your Mama?" Becca turned and pointed to her mother who was not far away and coming toward them. Becca looked back up into John's face and continued with her interview, "Are you going to your home, to see your Queen?" John smiled at her, "No, I'm going to a new country," Pointing out over the water he continued, "On the other side of the water." Becca's eyes grew wide. Looking at him again she placed her little hand on his cheek and asked with innocent curiosity, "Will the people there have white skin too?" He laughed, "Yes, some, but some will look like you and others are somewhere in between." By this time John's friends Steve and Boma had caught up with him and were leaning on the trunk they had been carrying for him. They too were smiling at the child's questions. Becca's mother was now ready to collect her daughter, "Come now Becca, say good-bye to Mr. John." She spoke in her native tongue. The little girl turned and wrapped her arms around his neck, "Why do you have to go?" John explained, "Well, I have work to do there." This didn't seem to quite satisfy the child, but her mother called her so she gave him a final hug and jumped off his knee. Taking her mother's hand she turned to him and waved a final farewell.

John stood as he watched the mother and daughter disappear into the crowd. Steve began talking as they picked up the trunk and followed John. "Maybe you find yourself a nice white girl over in America, Mr. John. " Boma replied, "I met a white girl once, almost married her." Steve was shaking his head, "Oh, really, what happened did she break out of her chains one night and run away from ya." Boma laughed, "No, I asked her if she would gain some weight for me, and she turned me down." Steve laughed heartily at the joke. John interjected, "Boma, you're all heart." Boma laughed again, but it was Steve who spoke next, "Ah, Boma, if you want the woman you got to speak to her heart, women want love like men want…" John broke in again, "Alright you two, that's enough." They were at the end of the dock now and set down the trunk. Boma, undaunted by his reprimand rang out, "Hey,

Mister John, we know God made men and women different, some of us just think they should be big differences." He lifted his hands up to his chest to portray large breasts and the two African's burst out laughing again. John smiled; he was going to miss them.

Turning his back to Steve and Boma he turned and gazed out over the waters. Something was beginning to stir within him and he wondered what it was. He had dreamt but could only remember pieces of it. Images of a green valley nestled within richly forested mountains. The vision seemed to pull back from his conscious mind, its vapor-like reality being difficult to grasp in the waking state. Steve called to him, and coming out of his reflections he realized it was time to get to the docks. He picked up his things and moved on.

A pair of moccasins padded softly through the woods. An American Native man danced on a high meadow that allowed an expansive view of a valley in the Pacific Northwest. His hands were raised and he was singing, his voice rising and falling to the distinct tempo of his people. He was calling on the Creator, to help, to send wisdom, to heal the land.

The wind blew with tempest strength and the scream of an eagle was heard. Opening his eyes toward heaven he saw the bird soaring high on the gusts that preceded a rolling herd of storm clouds. The trees around him bent and swayed, moaning as the wind forced a dance from their stiff members. His soul and spirit gathered all these sights and he nodded in acceptance of the answer to his prayers. And his mind was taken back, to a memory, only a few years before, but somehow he now understood that that night had been like this eagle, it rode on the winds of change drawing the attention of those who, without its presence, would never have looked up and noticed the coming storm.

What can I do?
What can I say?
He carved my path,
He made my way.

A loud pounding on the door woke Eve and her husband Josiah out of sleep. The house was dark but they made it out into the main room. Eve lit a lamp while Josiah answered the door. Josiah took a step back in surprise as Blue Cloud, a Native friend, stepped into the house. "I'm sorry to wake you up so late, but I need some help." A cry from the hallway told them one of the kids had been woken by the noise and Eve went to put the child back to sleep. Josiah thought there was trouble in the town and reached for his rifle. Blue Cloud grabbed his friends arm, "No, actually the trouble's in the village Josiah and I've come for Eve's help." Eve was just then stepping out of the hallway, "My help, how can I help?" Blue turned toward her, "It's Little Beaver, his nightmares have gotten worse, he's been having fits and not sleeping, they finally asked me what more we could do and well," He paused and eyed his friends thoughtfully, "I think you might be able to help Eve. " Josiah and Eve both looked at each other in complete amazement. Eve was shaking her head, "I don't know what else I can do Blue, we've prayed for him when they brought him to the mission" Blue Cloud interrupted her, "I thought perhaps you could come and spend the night with him Eve, maybe you'll catch his dreams."

Blue Clouds statement accosted Eve like a hit to the gut. She lowered herself slowly to the chair beside her. It seemed strange, the fact that the idea made sense to her. It had been awhile now, since her dreams had started: deep and intense visions, encounters of God. Her own tiny community and church had little wisdom to offer in such matters. In the Bible the many stories of dreams and those who had them encouraged her, but she found little instruction for how to walk through her visions, how to understand the figurative language of dreams.

A chance conversation about one of her night visions had been overheard by Blue Cloud one day, as he worked for her father at his ranch. Eve had never, before then, thought to seek his counsel on any matters. But Blue Cloud had been able to offer useful insight with his culture having a more open mindset about dreams, openly accepting things from the 'spirit world' in a way Eve's people seemed to fear. But Eve had been moved beyond her fears. She had, in her childhood been tormented by hellish nightmares. As she grew and sought after God and His salvation from such things, Jesus himself had invaded her dreams. He had taught her how to protect her dream life from intruders. *He had ridden toward her, breaking through clouds of light, on a white horse. He had given her gifts and reaching out his hand, without words, asked her to come with Him; beyond where she could see, into the clouds with Him. Eve had reached out her hand and taken the hand of Jesus. Her dream life had never been the same after that.*

Blue Cloud became her counselor and friend, not because he could always give an explanation, but because he offered that treasure of immeasurable value, he was never frightened by the dreams she shared with him and was able to see the hands of the Creator at work in it all. Eve's understanding of the language of dreams grew, and night by night over many years she became more and more exposed to the symbolic speech of images and visions that are the language of that illusive world.

Blue Cloud had never fully shared all he suspected Eve to be capable of, all that he believed she had been created to be. Some of her experiences amazed him and so now he stood in her living room, asking her for the first time to consciously attempt to use her gift.

Eve thought it sounded crazy, but a part of her she thought she had buried more deeply, rose up to the surface of her heart and began to move. She wanted to go and try. The thought of that small child being tormented in sleep, a torment she remembered well, stirred up her compassion and that vanquished all her fear. Sitting on her chair, she thought her mind should have been full of so many things, but all she felt was an urgency to be off. Eve looked up and saw Josiah and Blue gazing at her expectantly. Eve looked at her husband and asked, "Can I go?" Josiah set his gun down, this was not what he had expected when he had answered the door, but he had seen enough of what his wife had been going through to know this was not an evil design, but the hand of God, working outside of boxes men constructed of their cultures. He looked his wife squarely in the face and asked her one question, "Do you know what people might think?" Eve did. A white woman riding off with a Native man in the middle of the night could open them up to slander and censure. This was a good and right thing to do, but she was aware that it could be costly. She answered, "I'm only concerned about what you think Josiah; you are my husband." Josiah nodded, "Then you better go and see what God can do." Eve stood up and giving a quick glance to Blue Cloud turned to go get dressed.

Up until now, Eve's experiences had been pressed upon her; she had never willingly sought them out. As she dressed Eve's mind was filled with memories of her mother-in-law and the night she died. *Eve had sat up in her bed and seen a row of doors. The stars of the night sky were visible behind them. Eve realized she had been woken into this place by the sound of singing and looked as one of the doors opened and she saw her mother-in-law, Annie, step out of one door and be ushered into the other by spirits that were made of light. In the second room they brushed her hair and sang as she was prepared for what was coming. Eve sat in wonder, for Annie was young and whole and lovely beyond measure. When she was finished in the second room, she stepped out, clothed in light and came and spoke to Eve. Leaning over her bed in such a motherly way she had told Eve about the wonders of the other room she had been in. Tears like jewels flowed down her cheeks and Eve pulled her covers off and tried to go with her. Annie had tucked her back into bed and looking into her face had said, "No dear, you have to stay, for now." A call was made and a hand reached out and Annie turned to go through another vast door that appeared to be more like a gate.* Eve had then also been woken by a pounding on the door, and answering it was told by a family member that Annie had just passed away. She had been sickly and it was a blessing, but Eve had been given a glimpse of the truth, Annie hadn't just died, she had gone to heaven. As Eve did up the buttons of her dress she wondered if such a night as this was perhaps why she had to stay.

When she came out of her room, she found the living room empty. Grabbing her coat she stepped out the door and saw the light on in the barn, Blue Cloud and Josiah were saddling her horse. As she entered the yard she became aware of the immense vastness of the night sky above her. Looking up she felt very small in the company of those whose light was so bright she could perceive it even here from her little yard. Tonight though, she had the overwhelming understanding that they were gazing back at her.

It wasn't yet midnight and Blue Cloud stepped out of her barn just as she got there, Josiah leading her horse, Raven, just behind. Eve had a million thoughts suddenly race through her head. "Josiah, I don't know when I'll be back, so you'll need to see the kids off to school in the morning, will that be alright." Josiah smiled to himself, "Yes, I think I can handle it, for one day." Eve kissed him good-bye and stepped up onto Raven. Blue Cloud looked at her and nodding to Josiah turned and led Eve into the darkness.

A child cries within the night,
all seems dark; please grant us sight.

Eve sat on her horse, the night wrapping around her like a cold vice. She had no idea what was waiting for her when they reached the village, nor did she know how or if she may be able to help. Raven plodded faithfully on, following Blue Cloud's horse seemingly without question or fear. Eve wished she could feel so trusting. Her issue was not with Blue Cloud but with God. What was He doing to her now? She felt a pang of regret in the fact that she had never actually been to the village before. She had always thought she would like to go someday, but that day had simply never seemed to come. Now her course was set, in the middle of the night to go to the very place she had always hoped to, but never dared to enter in daylight. Eve found herself smiling as she realized this fit nicely into the pattern God had used in her dream life. Taking her in the night, through her dreams to new understandings, new revelations of who He was in ways she would never perceive in the light of the day.

Blue Cloud suddenly pulled his horse up and slid off quietly. Taking a hold of his rein and Raven's bridle he led the horses to a tree and tied them there. "We're almost there; I don't want to wake more people than we need to." Blue Cloud said. Eve followed him, but soon it was apparent that his thoughtfulness was not necessary. The areas in between the tepees had people sitting and standing around, obviously being kept awake by the cries of a child that could be heard nearby. Eve felt herself respond to the fervent cries, her body even aching to hold and comfort the little one. The whole place was filled with tension. Eve knew enough of her neighbors to understand that a child who could not be quiet was a danger to the whole tribe. From predators to enemies, these people relied on their ability to pass quietly and unnoticed through the countryside. Blue Cloud seemed to turn sharply away from the crying and just as Eve was about to ask him why she turned her gaze and found herself face to face with a man of seemingly great importance.

Eve suspected that this was the chief at first, yet soon dismissed the idea. He wore an air of self-importance, which seemed to exceed his actual station. He looked her over warily, took her hands and inspected them, he even touched a bit of her hair; he then flicked it back over her shoulder with a loud snort, this seeming to be all the communication necessary for him to express his disapproval. He and Blue Cloud then began to speak in their native tongue. Eve couldn't understand the speech, but she grasped enough of the tone of the conversation to realize he did not want her here. The conversation was brought to an end when a third man rose up and stood just beside the others. Eve felt all the humility that was due as she recognized this man was the chief. He was aging and wore a warm blanket over his shoulders, it was late and this was not a formal meeting so he wore no headdress or anything else that would have set his appearance apart from those around him. Yet, his presence carried a weight Eve had not encountered before. This man was king of his people and she was a foreigner whose admittance had not been granted his approval. He spoke a quick command and the two younger men stopped their bickering and Blue Cloud turned and made a formal introduction. "Eve Carson, this is our chief, Pale Moon, and this is our medicine man, Swift Horse." he motioned to the other who stood scowling at her. Eve realized she was completely unprepared to follow the appropriate protocol. Having no gift to present to the chief she felt herself fill with desperation, but it lasted only a moment as she was then flooded over with a glimmer of hope. As she looked into Pale Moon's face she saw a faint but warm and fatherly impression that soothed her and she dared to speak. "I am honored to meet you," she said to the chief, she felt her safest bet would be to ignore the other completely, "Please forgive me, I am not prepared to meet you," she said and clasped her hands in her embarrassment of them being empty before him, "I can only offer you my presence tonight and the help that may come with understanding what is troubling the child." As if on cue the night sky was filled with another deafening wail. Blue Cloud looked at her with a mild surprise and although Eve suspected the chief could understand English well, he translated what she had said. Pale Moon smiled slightly and looked to the disinterested party beside him and spoke, "She has come to us in a good way, let her stay and we will see." Without another word or look to Eve he turned back into his home. The other glowered at Blue Cloud and spat on the ground in front of them before stomping away.

Blue Cloud gave a short sigh of relief and led Eve on, this time straight toward the wailing.

Eve was able to smile slightly at the sight of familiar faces. She recognized the father, who was sitting outside the tepee and stood and opened the flap that served as the door for them without a word. The boy's mother got up and embraced Eve as soon as she saw her. Eve could feel a wave of relief wash over the woman and was amazed that it was her presence that had inspired it. Blue Cloud simply nodded to Eve as he took the mother out and she could hear the three of them speaking softly outside.

Eve gazed at the child who was at the moment apparently sleeping restlessly. She felt utterly lost and alone. What was she doing here, what was she supposed to do? Having absolutely no idea in or of herself, she knelt and prayed. "Dear Father, I need Your help, please. Don't let this child continue to suffer if help can be found. I need You now." Nothing appeared to happen. Eve knew God had heard her and had left her standing out on the edge of faith while she waited to see if God was actually going to show up. She pulled her legs around and sat beside the child. There was nothing else to do, but wait. Her heart went out to this little one, whose nights were full of so much terror. His parents had been attending church at the Mission for over a year now, with a few others, and it had been five months before that they had first sought prayer for their sons troubled nights. She placed her hand on his belly and began to sing softly. The atmosphere became other-worldly as peace fell around them.

Blue Cloud sent the mother and father off to have a break; they looked like they could sadly use one. If nothing else at least Eve could provide them one night's relief. When he looked in to check on her and the boy he saw Eve lying beside the boy singing softly. Positioning himself outside the door, where the father had been, he sat up and kept a prayerful vigil.

Eve hadn't believed in 'dream walkers' when Blue Cloud had first introduced her to the idea; that someone could walk around in the very dreamland that seemed so unique to each individual and yet interconnects all mankind by an elusive and unseen thread of common existence.

Dreams had become, however, a very real and constant way in which God revealed His love to Eve. Blue Cloud was an interesting individual to reckon with on the matter. He was a believer and follower of Jesus Christ, and allowed that relationship to expand and deepen his cultural belief's rather than dissolve them. The Bible was full of stories of divine communication through dreams, he saw people like Daniel as a dream walker. Daniel prayed, and God answered him by allowing him to see the king's dream. It seemed odd to him that Eve had such a hard time believing God would do a similar feat if they asked in good faith. Blue Cloud's wisdom on the matter and willingness to operate in this arena, or at least thrust Eve into operating in this arena spurred her on in a direction she was not entirely convinced she was ready for. Yet, there she lay, beside an innocent and troubled child; and her compassion had dared her to believe, and when she drifted off to sleep, she dreamt.

Snarls and howls rang out all around. At first she didn't recognize the sound of a child crying mingled in amongst the yips and wails of the coyotes. She turned toward the sound and saw the village before her. Images flashed of red eyes and fangs, people screaming, the sound of clothing being ripped. And all around the night was lit by a fire that raged. Eve ran through the tepee's following the sound of the crying. The realization that this was a dream budded in her understanding. She was also able to recognize that what she was seeing was real, it had significance to the physical world. Beside her stood an invisible man, he reminded her of Blue Cloud at times and he helped her navigate through the chaos and find her way.

Sitting alone outside his family's place sat the little boy, and Eve called his name, "Little Beaver!" He stopped crying and turned to the sound of her voice. Eve walked toward him and turned and looked at all he was watching. The flames burst in bright reds and oranges to fade into black, again and again giving light to different scenes of animals ravaging the place. The man beside her spoke, "He must learn to guard his dreams." Eve realized the simple lesson and wondered why she was being allowed to be a part of it.

She crouched down and took Little Beaver by the hands. He was barely four years old but he was strong, it was only his fear that was crippling him in his nightmares. Eve had learned this lesson herself and smiled as she knelt and looked in his eyes. "Little Beaver," she said coyly, "did you tell these coyotes they could come into your dreams?" The little one blinked back at her as if the question itself had taught him something. He looked around and shook his head –no- as he began to cry again. Eve reached up and touched his tears, "Well, they don't understand tears; you have to say it in a way they will hear." She stood up and turned, always looking at him to make sure he was watching carefully. She picked up a rock and tossed it gently in her hand, testing the weight before turning sharply and hurling it with great speed at the nearest animal. She hit it just in front of the hips and it spun around as it yelped in pain. She turned and flashed a smile at the little boy who was no longer crying but standing very still in shocked surprise. "Come on. I can't get them all by myself." Eve called as she picked up another stone to throw.

Little Beaver proved to have great aim and learned quickly. Eve kept instructing him with each stone. "You tell them to, 'Get out of here!'" Thunk-yelp. The boy followed suit, "Go away and never come back!" Eve smiled, he had spunk. Soon, however the coyotes left were staying out of range of the stones. Eve turned and placing her hands on her hips looked around. "Well, little man, I think we need something that'll reach a bit farther." She eyed the boy carefully. He glanced around and Eve watched as he reached for a stick on the ground. As his hand reached for a *weapon with more range his mind made it manifest, she saw the stick become an arrow and Beaver, picking it up, held a bow in his other hand. He had manifested what he needed. Eve nodded, he was lucid dreaming.*

His bow sang like a harp and soon it was raining arrows upon the intruders. When there were no more targets to aim at he lowered his bow and stood silently gazing at the quiet scene before him. Eve, prodded by the man beside her, knelt beside the boy. "Good job!" She said and he looked to her. When his face turned she saw a reflection in his eyes of a man dressed in white standing beside her. "Little Beaver," she said softly, "Do you see Him now?" The boy nodded. "Well, He's always been here, but when we get too afraid, we lose sight of him. Don't let anything ever block Him out, especially in this place. Only let things from Him come in here, everything else you drive right out of here. This is your dream land, it's a very special place where He'll come and talk to you, but you have to guard it, you have to fight for it like you just did, okay." Little Beaver looked around and the fires ebbed away and Eve felt warmth and light fill the place.

The boy was smiling and Eve was overwhelmed as she watched him run past her and into the arms of his heavenly Father. All light and love the Father glanced at Eve as He lifted the boy in his arms, and giving her a wink turned and began to talk to Little Beaver about cloud painting. The two were soon off into the sky and laughter resonated through the entire place.

Eve then felt as if she was being pulled from behind, out of somewhere. She had the faintest glimpse of a spherical orb and a man beside her whose presence was soothing, but before she could grasp that place she was thrown back into the reality of the dark tepee.

Eve gasped as she sat fully upright. Her mind reeled as it readjusted to receiving information through her body rather than her spirit. For a dreamer, waking can be the most jolting occurrence of the entire experience.

Blue Cloud must have heard her come out of sleep, for he was immediately beside her. "Eve." he whispered, "Are you alright." Her wide eyed and startled appearance gave him his first moment of hesitation that perhaps his idea hadn't been so good. Eve's eyes began to focus in the dim light that was coming in through the open flap behind Blue Cloud. Lying beside her, she saw Little Beaver sleeping peacefully. Eve let out a sigh and slumped into Blue Cloud's arms and hugged him. Looking up into his face she risked waking the boy as she exclaimed, "Oh my goodness, Blue, I can't believe God did that with me!" Blue hugged her but pulled back as if wanting to inspect her, "Are you sure you're alright?" Eve was laughing, it just bubbled over. She was completely overwhelmed, "Yes, yes, but no, I don't know." Eve stopped laughing as she realized something significant had happened, not just for Little Beaver, but for herself. Faith had stepped forward and blossomed into a divine experience and Eve was aware that she had been changed by it.

PART 2

Jesus answered and said to him,
"What I am doing you do not understand now,
but you will know after this." (c)

The speech is dark,
the meaning unclear
But I know I am loved,
when His song I do hear
Should I hope, should I fear,
the mystery of His plan?
Can I hold all this weight?
He's telling me I can.

Eve was dreaming again. She was happy, full of expectancy. She was dreaming of being a bride, anticipating her love to come and for them to be married. *Josiah came and embraced her. But she then found herself walking on a snowy path. She turned and laughed to him as he sat in a sleigh. "Just a minute, I'll gather a bouquet!" But as she turned she saw Blue Cloud, his hands in the flower bush, and he cut for her, two bouquets. Each one attached to a branch. The first one was short and the second one he handed her was longer. Eve was looking down at them in wonder when she heard a whoosh and turning she caught sight of Josiah waving good-bye as the sled drove off. He held the first, shorter bouquet and as the sled pulled away he tossed the flowers. Eve saw the lovely petals strewn about across the snow and wondered why he had ruined her bouquet. She didn't understand exactly what was happening but she knew she didn't want this. Everything within her screamed "Noooo!" and she tried to go after him, to reach for him, but she was held fast. Blue Cloud stood beside her and said something about*

her getting married and she looked down and realized she still held the
second bouquet.

Eve woke, emotions swirling turbulently around in her heart and mind. There would be no lingering under warm covers to ponder, no her morning was busy; she got up and quickly wrote the details of the dream down in her journal, then hurried to get breakfast going. Though it was early, the sun was up and the morning bright. Eve cracked the eggs and got the coffee started and happened to glance out the window and noticed their pigs were in the garden. She dropped her spoon in the sink and hurried into the bedroom. "Josiah! Wake up." He rolled over, "What is it?" She grabbed a shirt and handed it to him, "The pigs are out tearing through the garden." Josiah dropped his hands in defeat and lay a moment as he realized his day of rest was now lost.

Eve stood looking out the window, shaking her head. Her cabbages were ruined. Josiah emerged and stood behind her, getting a look out the window over her shoulder as he finished buttoning his shirt. He could only see a portion of the pig pen from this angle, but it was obvious they had torn down a whole corner, his day off would be completely eaten up fixing it. He sighed and poured himself a sip of coffee. Eve glanced at him; she hoped he'd get right out there and get them out before they destroyed anything else. Josiah saw her anxious looks and set his cup down. "Alright, I'll get out there." he said as he grabbed her by the waist and turned her around. "But you know this isn't exactly how I was hoping to spend my morning." He said as he buried his face into her neck and pulled her close. She smiled, enjoying the moment, but when he lingered she pulled back, "Go on, with you." He sighed. She gave him a kiss and he stepped back. Grabbing his hat, "Alright, I'd better get out there and keep my critters in line."

Eve was turning toward the sink again as he finished his remark and gave her a playful smack on the rump. Eve turned to get after him, but he ducked out the door laughing.

Eve turned and looked out the window with a sigh, she could go out and help him. She realized it was time, Josiah had been wanting to stop raising pigs for a while, the destruction of the garden now seemed the last straw and Eve decided to tell him when she went outside that he could sell them off.

Life kept moving, the demands of the day often driving her dreams from her mind so some days were easier than others. But not this day, this was one of those days in which Eve was troubled by things she alone had seen. That morning her dream had taken her into deep water. *She was floating in the depths, with the invisible man beside her, as usual. She wasn't struggling or reaching for the surface, trying for air, she was simply hovering. She could see a land formation nearby and once she was calm and accepting of her surroundings, they began to change. A cloud of silt from the sea bed began to rise, as something large was disturbing the bottom. Eve watched as a serpentine creature rose from the depths. The body glimmered like silver in the water, and the head moved toward her. Just when she began to fear this monster may devour her, it spoke.*

"There are many things, ancient and forgotten things, that are about to be awakened. You are going to see them awaken." Eve blinked in amazement; the voice was deep and penetrating and had a foreign accent. It turned and swam toward the land and she awoke.

Josiah stepped into the house. The morning sun filled the place and Eve was hurrying the kids out of their rooms. She was bustling about, telling one to put his shoes on and another to wash their hands all the while trying to place one last pin in her own hair. Josiah stood patiently, he could see she was trying to hurry, but he did hate walking into church late.

At last they were all piled in the wagon and on their way. After they had a good piece of road behind them Josiah reached over and took Eve's hand. "How're you doing?" Eve felt pulled back to reality by the question. "I'm fine, why?" Josiah lifted her hand and kissed it, "You've just been quiet, that's all." Eve turned her gaze back to the forests and fields around them. "Oh, just thinking I guess. I had a bit of a strange dream." Josiah smiled and nodded. 'A strange dream,' Eve seemed to have a lot of those.

Eve tried to relax and enjoy the fellowship of her church family that morning, though her heart was uneasy. It wasn't just this morning's dream; many of her dreams lately had left this odd aftertaste in her soul that she just couldn't seem to shake off. She felt desperate, desperate for God, for His presence that would calm all her unrest. While the choir led the congregation in the closing hymn Eve sat, praying quietly, letting her tears flow.

Rising Eve dried her face and hoped they could get home quickly. She had learned it was easier to get by if others didn't see her tears. Exhaustion frayed the edges of her heart. They were mingling and saying hellos and good byes, how are you's, and nice to see you's; when she caught Miss Ruth's eye. Miss Ruth was in her late fifties or early sixties Eve reasoned. She had come to Frontier a little over four years before and had been quite the talk of the town. Being a woman traveling west alone, was enough to make her interesting, her beautiful ebony skin, though, gave her another level of distinction. Ruth was large and loud, but in a wonderful way that had instantly endeared her to Eve.

Ruth caught the eye of her young friend and flashed a smile that dried what remained of Eve's tears. She walked over and being quite a bit taller than Ruth, let herself fall into the comforting embrace of her friend. Eve loved her hugs, Miss Ruth would hold her till any heartache or trial simply got squeezed out of her existence. "Lord bless me, how you doing?" Ruth said as she stepped back and Eve straightened up. Eve looked at her and tried to speak, "Good and how are you?" but no words came. Eve choked on a swell of something that rose up within her that was beyond articulation. Her lips trembled and tears anew threatened to flow. Miss Ruth didn't wait any longer and grabbed Eve into another bear hug again, this time speaking into her friend's ear, "That's alright child, I can see you's troubled and now ain't the time. You come see me this week alright and we'll sort it all out." She stood back and looked into Eve's face, "Just like a load o dirty laundry, we'll get it all sorted." Eve was nodding and finally managed a, "Yes." Ruth smiled and nodded, she could see Eve needed some form of relief for whatever she was going through. "Alright." she agreed and clasped Eve's hand in her own. That simple act melted Eve's loneliness as she moved through the crowd of people she knew and loved but who did not know of the deep craters of hurt God's footprints were leaving as He walked in her heart.

That evening, Josiah sat reading while the kids played in the orange glow of the sunset. After she had finished the dinner dishes Eve grabbed her shawl and wrapped it around her shoulders. She passed Josiah and walked through the yard. Her husband noticed her but turned back to his book. He knew his wife was a sensitive spirit, artistic in her understanding. Over the years he had come to learn that the best fix for her heavy heart was a solitary walk and talk with God.

Eve wandered through the yard letting her hand touch the fence. She came to the horse corral. Raven nickered softly and came to her. Eve patted her nose and smiled as the animal turned away once it discovered Eve had no treats for it. Eve watched the graceful movement of her horse, the beauty of the swish of its tail. She sighed and turned, leaning her back against the fence. She didn't have enough time to walk up the hill behind the house to her wild meadow sanctuary, the sun was fading too quickly. Instead she contented herself with the sight of her humble home. Her little family made a sweet picture, the boys were playing with sticks and hollering while the dog barked and bounded along with them. Her daughter sat on the steps next to her father's knee, sketching the chickens in the yard. Eve sighed; she had so much to be thankful for. Her life was truly blessed, why then, dear God was her heart not settling into rest? She was happily married to a man whom she loved and who loved her. Her children were good natured and healthy, she knew the Lord and was aware of His great love for her, what more could there be? Eve didn't know the answer to her question yet, but her heart seemed to be aware that God was trying to tell her that there was something more. At the moment Eve was allowing the blessedness of her present situation to shield her from the knowledge of anything else, even words from God's own lips.

I heard what You said,
still You say it again.
Pushing Your will,
showing Your plan.
Can I understand,
all that I see?
Can I comprehend,
You're showing me, me?

Light and mist filled the area around her and Eve turned and saw a native woman, who seemed to be her sister in this place, being washed and dressed for her wedding. She smiled and was filled with joyful anticipation. Then the women doing the washing came and began to work on her as well.

Eve saw her father and he handed her two scrolls. Eve unrolled them and looked, they were written in a strange and ancient language, but she was able to recognize her father's handwriting. One of the scrolls, like the bouquets from her other dream, was smaller than the other. She rolled them up and tried to leave, to get away from this situation, although she kept the scrolls with her. Try as she might to get away she sensed she was simply going around in circles. Around and around she went, being confronted by things she could not tolerate or seem to care for but she found no way out.

The wedding preparations were still going on and finally she decided to go and help the others. As she did so Eve noticed a man standing to the *side, watching her from a distance. His presence seemed to calm her and she even smiled as she worked.*

Then the messengers came, speaking of her father and hadn't she received the first message, for he was sending a second message. Eve wondered what the message was and ran after the messenger, hoping to ask him. Her father met her and they walked and began speaking about the two scrolls.

Eve drifted slowly into consciousness; the warmth of the light in the dream filling her soul and causing her to try to linger in sleep. She rolled onto her back and lay blinking at the ceiling as she relived the dream now in the memory of her waking mind. The two scrolls had been contracts, with signatures at the bottom. Their golden ink and strange penmanship seemed ingrained in her head. It was important. Important enough to cause her to brave the cold air outside her covers so that she could write it down before any details faded.

As Eve watched her pen move across the page of her journal, she remembered a man who had come to town a year or so before with a cart full of the 'latest' fashions and inventions for sale. One that had caught her eye during his demonstration was 'invisible ink'. The salesman wrote a word out for all to see and soon the ink dried and vanished from sight. After a moment or two the man applied another substance that caused the writing to reappear. Now as Eve penned her dream out she considered how very much her dreams were like 'invisible ink'. She had learned to write them down, for her memory of them soon faded and was lost. If she journaled them it helped her remember them better and it left a record that she could reference later. This was one of those instances when she felt very thankful for her discipline of keeping a dream journal. As she wrote down the main details and went to describe the scrolls she found herself calling them 'two marriage contracts'. This surprised her, for although that was what they had been she had not seen them as that exactly until she had written it down in black and white. Her pen stopped as she sat alone and motionless in her little kitchen the rest of her family still perhaps in that dreamland that she had exited.

'Is God telling me I will have a second marriage?' she silently wondered to herself. It wasn't a strange thought for a woman whose husband worked in the silver mine which was hard and dangerous work. But this was more than fearful feminine reasoning. Eve was pondering whether or not God was trying to let her know, to prepare her, for a life beyond the one she now knew. Anxiety began to rise up within her causing her heart to work harder than it needed to. "Dear God," she prayed, "Please tell me this is not so." The core of her being reached out to God like a child reaches to be lifted up by a parent. Eve heard no reply, but visions, scenes from another dream she had recently, began to flood her mind. The images of the wedding bouquets, two wedding bouquets, like the two scrolls, both being handed to her. from people she loved and trusted. In one dream it was Blue Cloud, in this one her father. Eve flipped the pages of her journal back and found the dream of the flowers. It occurred to her that the same message was communicated in both dreams, just in different forms. Eve turned the pages forward and re-read the words she had just written. 'They were sad I had not received the first message, so they told me he had sent a second…' Eve was hit with the realization that the 'messages' referred to were her dreams. She had not understood the meaning of the bouquets, or had not been willing to understand it, so she had been sent another message, another dream. Eve's emotions quickly began to overrun her thought process, her rational mind going to war against her sensitive heart. Shock, anger, disbelief, shock again, then a sweet brush of love. Eve could faintly see that the unwelcomed understanding was infused with potent love, but her heart was too full of fear to be touched by it.

Who else hears the things He says,
Days come and go but His word stays.

Night by night the dreams continued and Eve was surprised by the ebb and flow of divine truth and love that was continually penetrating within her heart and mind. It was a morning like any other, but Eve was troubled and decided to ride over to her father's house as soon as Josiah and the kids were out the door.

The sun shone through the trees as the slightest hints of color were appearing on the leaves. Eve was thankful she had thought to put on her warmer jacket for the ride. It would be quite hot this afternoon but Fall was here and the air held a cool crispness to it well past midday. Raven clip-clopped beneath her and Eve resolved to not be shaken. She had decided, so many years ago, to follow God. Now, if He led her into something that may be unpleasant, would she pull back and cease to follow Him? She was pondering so much of what God's true character was like, that she nearly missed the fact that it was her character that was being tested. She had experienced too much to easily discredit a divine visitation albeit through a dream. She had learned to fight to keep her heart and mind, whether sleeping or awake, free from evil intruders. But her own reaction, her own thoughts, when confronted by the discernable message disturbed her. She knew she didn't have all of the pieces to the puzzle, but what she could see was shaping up to look like something she would really rather not look at.

Raven could sense the tension in her rider and as Eve's thoughts raced she found her horse racing as well. Eve didn't rein her in. The thundering sound of the hooves and the cool slap of the wind against her face forced her to concentrate on the 'now'. She was only a quarter of a mile from her father's cabin and she let Raven fly. Eve was a bit breathless as she pulled up. She was breathing hard, her eyes red from tears and wind. Yet, she found herself still here, still conscious of this communication of a promise that could only be realized by going through something painful.

She tied Raven to the rail fence and tried not to notice that her hands were shaking. She patted her horse thinking she should perhaps cool her off, but Raven's breathing was steady and she seemed content to stand and rest.

Looking around Eve realized the buggy was gone which meant her mother, at least, and perhaps her father as well were not at home. That was just as well. She had really come here, hoping to find Blue Cloud as he had been working for her dad on the new barn for over a month now, so she headed in that direction. If her dad was at home he'd be out there by now anyway.

Eve found Blue Cloud working on the stall doors just as she had suspected. She had hoped to see her folks, but was a bit relieved that no one else seemed to be around. She wanted to ask Blue Cloud about her dreams.

"Eve," Blue Cloud called when he saw her coming into the barn. The siding was only up on one side and the stalls were only framed up, but she nodded as she looked around. Dad and Blue should have it finished before it snowed. "Hi Blue." Eve called back. He kept working as she walked over.

He had a nail in his lip and was lifting a board up into position. When he grabbed the nail out of his mouth he told her, "You're parents went into town today I expect they'll be gone for a while." Eve smiled and fumbled a bit with how to begin, "Oh," she said then added, "Well, actually, it's you I've come to see." Blue Cloud finished pounding the nail and took a good look at his friend. He could tell right away that she was troubled. He placed the hammer down and pointed for her to have seat on a bale of hay while he continued to sort boards. He'd listen while he worked without the pounding of a hammer for a bit.

Eve sat and rubbed her hands on her skirt. Her emotions were on the verge of spilling over. She thought she might know something, a terrible and new something, how could she explain it? "Well," she began, "I've been dreaming." Blue Cloud gave her a familiar look that said, 'no kidding, you?' without a word. Eve shook her head at him feeling silly and defeated already. She went on, "Have you ever had a dream repeat?" Blue Cloud nodded. "I've had nightmares reoccur." he stated. Eve shook her head, "Me too. No, this wasn't a nightmare; it was a 'God' dream. I didn't understand the first one, so I had a second, similar yet different dream that caused me to understand that God may be…" Eve didn't realize she had stopped talking. Her eyes had strayed out the window as she searched for the right words only to discover that there were no 'right words' for this. "Well, what I mean is that the same 'message' seems to be coming to me again and again, in different ways." Her mind filled with other images from countless dreams and she couldn't help but be overwhelmed by the realization that God had been trying to breach a topic with her for some time, but she had refused to consider it, until now. Emotions rose up despite her wish to keep them under wraps and she put a hand to her mouth. She couldn't speak it. She absolutely refused to even allow herself to make any part of it real in this waking world, even by mere words.

Blue Cloud's face showed real concern. She now had his full attention. He sat on a small ladder and said her name, "Eve."

Eve turned toward him her eyes glossy with tears. "Why would he tell me this?" She spoke softly as a tear dared to run down her cheek. She didn't want to be here, she didn't want to think about this let alone talk about it. She stubbornly wiped the tear from her face. "I know my fears. I know what it is to be caught in that trap, but this is something different. This is from Him, and He won't let me go."

Blue Cloud looked out the open walls thoughtfully. But it wasn't long before he spoke, "Well, Eve, whatever it is that is troubling you, it's obviously a hard topic for you to consider, but you should consider this. You hear from the Creator, how would you feel if He didn't tell you about something that could affect you so deeply?"

The growth of her anger was stunted for the moment as she considered this. Her fear was based in losing Josiah whether by death or some strange turn of events that would lead to divorce. The second was improbable; they adored each other, while the first remained unthinkable.

The truth of the matter was that death and heartache occurred. God promised that His path lead to eternal glory not that there wouldn't be stones along the way or even abrupt turns. Eve was humbled as she saw her own lack of character. She caught a bitter glimpse of herself. She was confronted by the truth that even after years of God speaking to her in such a real and intimate way, she could become angry to the point of forsaking Him if He chose to allow such a drastic change to occur while leaving her unaware. Still, she considered these feelings wrong, for sadness came to mankind every day. Who was she to receive such communication? None the less, the message had come, and more than that, she could comprehend it. Her reasoning mind could not come to terms with all the why's and what for's of the matter, for such things she had to rely on faith. Could she trust God? He knew best; and if He was choosing to tell her of something before it happened He had a good reason for doing so.

She sat and pondered all this, her heart suddenly stripped and empty of all feeling. She had nothing with which to rebuke God. She didn't feel the need to share more with Blue Cloud at the moment, he had given her the counsel she had needed. Her fear of one loss had momentarily been wiped away by her fear of a greater loss. Of course, the end of her marriage would be terrible but, what if she lost her soul instead? Eve was forced to look upon her heart and realize that although she loved Josiah very dearly, she loved her God more. What she and Josiah had was temporal, mortal. It was an important and pivotal part of her life, but it was God who held her identity, it was God who offered her true life beyond this dimly lit existence. She saw now that her devotion was being tested by that terrible beauty of divine perspective that surpasses time.

Blue Cloud had gone back to work this time feeling free to pound in nails again. Sighing, Eve stood, suddenly wanting to be home. She could always count on Blue Cloud to put things in perspective for her. Eve watched him for a moment, caught his eye and waved a thank you before heading out. Blue Cloud watched her walk away, and for a moment he was aware of a sweet sadness that hung in the atmosphere of the place where Eve had taken a small step toward deciding to accept the will of her Maker

PART 3

*Now I tell you before it comes,
that when it does come to pass,
you may believe that I am He.* (d)

In a land, built on change,
things familiar still seem strange
Hammer and nail, wood and stone,
yet, no place to call his own.
And still he works to bring them hope;
he is the help that lets them cope.
As time ticks on he'll start to see,
a vapor promise of what could be.

Dust was hanging throughout the air, as the sun shone in the room it gave the atmosphere a very golden hue. John Bates hardly noticed how bright it made the place appear as he walked in. Though his clothes were dirty, he sat on a crate in the large canvas tent that was his home and began unwrapping his right wrist. The sound of construction rang out in the distance and all around, as if he was sitting in the center of a clanging symphony. His ears had all but gone deaf to the sound.

Sighing, he yanked and pulled at the cloth bandage that seemed unwilling to let loose of his hand. The wound frustrated him. It wasn't anything to worry about, and yet it had kept him from doing much of the work he was accustomed to. As an engineer he knew he didn't have to dirty his hands in the building of dams and bridges, yet he enjoyed knowing he had helped 'build' something. Thoughts and designs seemed such an intangible beginning toward something greater. His favorite moment was taking those first steps onto a bridge, being able to walk from one place to another, where there had been no way before.

Turning his wrist he winced slightly, there was one degree of healing that had not finished its work yet. The cut at the lower end of his palm had healed nicely; he only had to wait to regain a bit more mobility. He looked out the open tent flap. He could see people bustling about. The bridge which was his current project was coming along nicely and the nearby town was churning with anticipation. It would allow supplies and trade to move much more freely with the larger towns to the east.

Standing, he moved to the opening and stood looking out at the pine forest that was split in two by the rushing water. The people here fascinated him. He could see so much of the influence of the lands they came from. In the six months he had been there he had enjoyed the cuisine of more lands than he had experienced in his travels. Swedish, Chinese, Italian, German, even good English meals; yet everything absorbed the rustic flavor of the land around it. You were aware it came from another place, and yet this land had somehow claimed it as its own as well. Everyone he had met seemed to belong here.

America was this new land, full of possibility, yet the price for that hope and dream was high. Doctors were scarce and sickness deadly. Cultural misunderstandings were rampant as people from all around the world fought for their right to carve out a new life for themselves. Yet, here he was, a welcomed visitor. His work made him a valuable commodity, yet he felt aloof, not really one of them. He was beginning to long for a place to call home and he wondered if he could find it somewhere in this vast land.

"Hey, Mr. Bates!" his foreman yelled. John turned away from the wilderness and saw Parker weaving his way toward him through the construction camp. "Paul is having a problem out at the 23rd piling, thought you'd better come have a look!" John nodded and looked down at his hand; he could do without the bandage now. "I'll be right there." he said as he reached in for a fresh shirt and headed back to work.

The truth you speak, it holds me fast
For my life, your die is cast
Strong bars, divine, have built my cage
His speech pours out, and fuels my rage.

A *sound like rolling thunder woke Eve into a dream. Light was everywhere and she stepped into it. Her old house, where she had lived in her youth, materialized around her. Her sisters and mother were there. There was talk about tending the garden and she saw her mother step outside. The rumbling sound grew louder and Eve stepped to the window so she could see what was making the noise, what she saw disturbed her terribly.*

Three large teams pulling gigantic plows were tearing up her lovely bit of wilderness garden in the back yard. Her roses and wild grasses were being destroyed and a dark rich soil was leveled. Eve ran outside to her mother and found her working in a side garden bed. The vision of her mother wiped the sweat from her brow as Eve hurried up to her. "MOTHER!" Eve screamed and pointed, her mother seemed completely calm. "Yes dear, it's alright, they are from the insurance agency, the believer's assurance agency, they are here to see to our investment." Eve shook her head, she couldn't understand what her mother was talking about, but it became quite clear that their work was sanctioned and if her mother was allowing it, Eve could not stop it.

She was then asked to serve tea on the porch to the very ones who had been tearing up her garden. She stood to the side with arms crossed and listened to their conversation. One was a woman, who reminded her of

Miss Ruth. The other one, Eve was amazed to see was Blue Cloud and the third man she couldn't make out clearly. They sat and chatted with her mother about an upcoming dance, and how it would be a great opportunity for Eve to meet a potential husband. The idea was absurd. Eve was totally aware of her husband, Josiah, and her home. In fact she tried to wake herself from the dream repeatedly, but seemed only to flicker through light and find herself still in the dream. The others continued laughing and talking in front of her and Eve finally interrupted and spoke to her mother. "I want to go home," she stated and tears began to form in her eyes, "I don't want to go to another place and meet someone else." Her mother just looked at her, a deep penetrating gaze and said, "Yes you will, dear." Her voice was filled to the brim with understanding, which simply infuriated Eve all the more. She felt the strong resolve of her own will solidify within her and she shouted, "But I've never been unhappy! He's a good man, he's done nothing wrong!" Eve flung her arm toward the tilled earth that was her heart, which now lay broken and bare by the will of someone far greater than herself. She knew exactly what she was being shown, and she didn't like it one little bit, and she definitely didn't want to accept it.

Again she tried to pull herself from the vision, but she seemed to be held fast. Her mother looked at her and Eve felt lost in her eyes, so full of compassion and understanding, and yet also encased in a firm resolve that could not be moved. Eve burst into sobs and her mother's arms caught her and held her. Beyond all reason, Eve was comforted by a truer love than she had ever known.

Eve woke and grasped her covers. Her mind reeled as the reality of the present and the truth of what she had just experienced flooded her consciousness simultaneously. Her heart had been pried open and she struggled to close the tear in the comfort of the 'now', but she couldn't. The pain was intense and raw, but she found that the pain did not reach to her arms and legs, so she got up. Dreams often faded as she went on about her day, this one though she soon found was different. She moved through her morning automatically, the routine of breakfast and getting the kids dressed and kissing everyone as they went out the door passed by but her heartache remained.

Once she found herself alone in the house she began to pace. She couldn't accept it, and yet try as she might, she could not un-know it. She stood before a precipice of choice; to accept what God was telling her, or deny it. Bitterness welled up in her throat like bile. Her reasonable mind could not undo all the links and circumstances, divine encounters, and actual Godly love that had brought her to this point. And she realized she had no power to change God's will. She was humbled as she contemplated how small she was in His hands. How she proceeded now would only change how she would be affected by the unfolding of His will.

The promise was that she would be blessed by this dramatic alteration, a fuller life, a joy full life. Becoming a soul willing and able to accept even the hard things from God as gift and be thankful for them. But her doubt rose up in a desperate attempt at self- preservation and she staggered on the edge of becoming a soul riddled with disbelief, discontent, and bitterness. The realization surfaced ominously that she could be ruined by her own disillusions about what is good. Her mind continued to churn God's words to her over and over. How could such pain come from a good God? Again she prayed for a release from fear, that if this wasn't from Him it would fade away, and again there was only a 'stillness' given to her as an answer as all she had heard in her heart and soul from her Maker remained standing, immovable, within her.

She bowed her head and closed her eyes, but the ache was still there. Her heart was raw with the intense emotion of the dream; wanting Josiah, not being able to get back to him, being held in the firm grasp of Providence. How could this be, her worst fears not only to be allowed by God, but to be the very working of His own hands?

Eve stood at the window, the wintery landscape painted a chilling reflection of the icy sorrow that was sweeping across her soul. Days came and went; the children grew another inch or two, evidenced by the marks on the doorpost. She lived and loved and laughed, like always and yet secretly, inwardly, she walked in a grief no one else could comprehend, and her relationship with God deepened in that season for God was the only one who knew completely what she was going through. She was a witness bound, bound to carry a burden that was hers alone. She searched the scriptures for proof. She wanted definitive evidence that a good and loving God would not orchestrate something so hurtful for one of his own children. But in the pages of scripture she found again and again tales of Divine love carrying His people *through* such difficulties. Joseph was betrayed and imprisoned, but saved his family. Hosea was commanded to marry a prostitute, his marriage not designed to be a happily ever after, but an illustration of redemption after loss. But it was when she found herself reading of the prophet Ezekiel and how God told him what He was going to do and then took his wife, Eve slammed her Bible shut.

She sat there, staring at the Book. The Book that held so many promises, the hope for mankind and now it pained her. It wasn't that there was no hope, she was now simply being confronted by the cost of it, the price she was being asked to pay seemed high indeed.

Light fell upon the table and she sunk back in her chair. How could she judge this? She knew of missionaries who suffered greatly. Women lost husbands and husbands lost wives every day without warning or reason from their Maker. Her eyes drifted out to the sea of blue sky that floated above her home. If He was going to take this much from her, He was also giving her much as well. A slight smile etched across her face despite all the tantrums of her heart and mind, there was something planted deeper still, something that knew God and refused to deny Him her good opinion. He was asking something of her she knew it. He was asking her if she would willingly accept this from Him. Tears that glowed with the heavenly hues of the distant sunset were the only physical evidence of her response.

So this is love?

Eve was trying to run, but hot tears filled her eyes and rocks and sticks seemed to grab at her feet. It was now mid-winter again, and her dreams were doing their work. She felt like a prisoner to the apparently iron resolve of a Creator who was holding her in His immeasurable hands. She was trying to escape, from Him, from what she didn't want to know. She wanted to hate God for what He was doing, but He was doing it in such a way that she was ever aware that what He was doing to her, He was also doing for her.

She followed her well-worn path through the woods. The deer trail was pressed into the few inches of snow that lay resting in the forest. On any other day she might have been taken by the serene beauty and quiet of the icy wilderness around her.

Visions from her dream this morning kept flashing through her mind. She couldn't stop the images from repeating. *Josiah knocked down, a pool of blood, his hand motionless and pale…two song birds winging and singing, one suddenly ripped out of the air by a ferocious crow… Josiah standing at a doorway to heaven, basked in light and love, smiling then turning to go.* Each dream was a parable of the same scenario, again and again she witnessed it and yet woke to another truth; to the reality that Josiah was alive and well and no visible obstacle could be seen to affront their happiness.

47

Eve stumbled up the next turn of the hill and stopped. Before her the trees parted and a meadow slumbered beneath the cold of winter. Catching her breath she walked on. Her tears cooled her face as the cold air chilled the watery streaks. The snow crunched under her boots and when she tired of the sound she stopped and gazed out over the valley below. She didn't often come up here in the winter and she was struck by the size of the dam, how well defined the path of the river appeared. Eve calmed down enough so that she was able to perceive a presence nearby and when she turned she noticed that Blue Cloud was squatting, wrapped in a deer hide, looking down over the valley as well.

Feelings flooded over her again at the thought that his presence was no accident here, that though this was a surprise it was also an appointment. Although she could see how it could be a much needed release to share some of her burden, speech alone could not communicate all she had experienced and she shuddered at the thought of trying to express what she was going through.

Terror was no stranger to her. She knew how it could take hold of a person. But this was different, she wasn't experiencing fear brought on by her own mortal shortcomings and concerns. At night, while sleeping, God was pressing hard truth on her, always the hard visions were paired with a glimpse into heaven such that awe and wonder of things beyond consumed her and she could not doubt that she was in an ongoing conversation with her Creator. She prayed, but she never prayed for the visions to stop, only that God would take away anything that was not of Him…and the dreams still came, the message the same.

She turned her head and committed herself to the vista again. And the two friends remained in that attitude for some time, despite the fact that they were both aware of each other's presence.

Finally, it was Blue Cloud who first broke the solemn silence. "I suspect we are both here for a similar reason." He stated sadly as he stood. He lowered his head to his chest and closed his eyes, he seemed troubled and Eve wondered why. He turned and almost silently walked across the snow towards her.

Eve cheeks were still being washed by cascading tears that she was unable to stop. Blue Cloud noticed these and drawing up beside her turned his gaze to the valley alongside his friend.

He lowered his head slightly toward her and spoke softly, "How are you Eve?"

She lowered her eyes as she struggled to keep it together. Shaking her head she lifted it and tried to speak, "Not so good lately. And yet, I'm fine." The truth of her statement was an irritation, she was fine, she was functioning, this hurt but it was not destroying her and part of her resented that. She found herself wondering why Blue Cloud was here and decided that an interest in his day may be a welcomed distraction to hers. "Why are you here?" she asked.

Blue looked around, as if he could see spirits that were surrounding them, "My visions have been troubling me lately, I come here to seek the Great Spirit." As he said this he looked into Eve's eyes and she knew that he could see in her a similar need for comfort from the very One who brought them such troubles.

She let out a laugh and words flowed out of her in broken lines of speech, "It's the same with me, I see hard things… that I would rather have not seen." She tightened her arms in front of her against the cold. "And I'm afraid of the depth of my anger. I'm experiencing sorrow and pain that are real, and then I wake to find out that it was just a dream and I..." she found her whole body trembling with rage, "and I'm angry at the way He's..."words failed her and she grew silent.

Blue Cloud responded, "Since when are your dreams 'just dreams' Eve?"

Eve lifted her chin in slight defiance as she acknowledged the truth, "Since they have become painful and hard to accept, I know I shouldn't deny they are from Him ..., but I suppose I find it comforting, to think perhaps it's just my imagination, it's just me."

Blue Cloud felt a bit concerned over her state of mind. "But only for a time." It was a statement, but it sounded like a question as well.

Eve knew it was true. "Yes, only for a time. Just when I think I can't take any more of God's terrible beauty, He reveals His heart to me, and I am able to swallow the bitter tasting truth and the reality that is...God." Even as she said the words, Eve's heart raged within her and she turned toward her friend, "Still, how...?" Eve stumbled and her fist braced against Blue Clouds' chest, he grabbed her elbow and tried to steady her. She shook her head and thumped his chest again. He was real, he was here, she was awake. Yet, the truth remained, still she *knew*. She spoke through tears of hot anger, "How...this is not what I want, I don't want...what kind of love is this?" Images of her dreams flashed upon her consciousness again. *She sat on the chair and pulled her children close and wiped a tear from her face and started; "Now I have to tell you, Daddy's had an accident."* Her chin sunk to her chest and she cried. She felt she shouldn't indulge such emotions, feel such grief when the present circumstances didn't yet call for it, and yet with her dreams, the very things that were to be a vessel of hope and communion with the Divine, she was being thrust into a grief she could not escape. Her knees buckled and she let them, Blue Cloud held her hands and she held onto him. Into the frigid air Eve's voice erupted leaving a trail of vapor behind it as it traveled up toward heaven, "HOW CAN THIS…. BE LOVE?!"

Eve sobbed uncontrollably and considered she could be going mad. But it wasn't her reason and mind that was out of control, no. She could look at all she had been shown and understand God was going to take her husband, people died every day. Yet, He was telling her He was going to do it. He must have a reason she couldn't see, but she did trust. It was her emotions that were overwhelming her. Blue Cloud rested on his knees in front of her, as her sobs ebbed away and she felt that unexplainable calm that washes over once you've let yourself fully *feel*.

Blue Cloud spoke, "You don't know who you are, Eve. God shows His love to us by breaking his children, is this not what He did with His Son the Christ?"

Eve nodded but looked away, the cool of the air calming the flush of her face. Her hair was loose and as it lay down her back nearly to her waist, a strand was caught in the wind and trailed in the air in between her and Blue Cloud.

Blue Cloud reached up and took hold of the lock and began speaking, "I dreamt once that the East Wind was an English lady. She stood gazing out over a hill to this vast land, and when two braves came upon her, rather than killing her they were enraptured by her golden hair." Blue Cloud looked up and Eve wondered what he was seeing. In that moment he looked old, his eyes dark and ancient. He went on, "My people are like the wild grasses and flowers of this land, and many of us have been trampled by the armies and power of the whites, yet we must make our peace with the Great Spirit for his hand in letting them come to us. But in their wake has come that East Wind; that gentle touch that lifts the scent of the flowers and grasses and dances with them, becomes a part of them and makes something new." He was still holding her hair, "I remember your grandmother, the one that was of my people Eve I know you wish you would have known her, but God has awakened in you all that is good in the two peoples who have attributed to your existence. You are that bit of East Wind that lingered here and is lovely." He held up the lock of her hair as if it was proof of what he said. "The world is full of war and misunderstanding, brothers kill brothers as it has been since the beginning. But it is people like you who are a blending, who are a testament that we can come together in love and understanding that the world needs. His plans for you may still be hidden from view behind the cloud. You must understand that your cloud is large and heavy for it is perhaps bringing behind it a destiny just as large and bright."

Eve shook her head, "I'm nobody." She looked up through reddened eyes, "My days are spent mending clothes and feeding chickens, I live in a tiny little house at the edge of the world." She shook her head, her petitions sounding tired, even to her own ears.

Blue Cloud laughed at her, "Your argument is not good, Eve. You may live in a tiny house at the edge of the world, but over that edge, you also live at the edge of the spirit world."

Eve sighed, "I wish it was simply a matter of great works, but He's not just telling me do this or do that. He's messing with my heart. I'm caught in a tragic romance, not a holy calling, Blue Cloud." She said in a tired sad voice. She couldn't fight anymore, her energies were spent and she just wanted to go home.

"Perhaps, they are one in the same." He said softly. But Eve had risen and started to walk away, so she did not hear him.

The sun shone brightly on the day she buried Josiah. As she walked across her front porch in the heat, she passed by the rose bush that had been planted by the front door. Josiah had bought it for her on their tenth anniversary. It had given one lovely bloom, but in the nearly three years since it had been tormented by neighbor's dogs, the goats and a very dry summer. Eve had left it alone, hoping that it would come back, believing it could be a symbol that her marriage to Josiah could still have life. And it had become such a symbol, just not the one she had wanted. This spring it remained a dead stick, with no new life sprouting. She had dreamt weeks before...*of walking by it and God standing there, pointing to it, "You know you need to dig that up." And Eve had, in the dream, and then amazingly a new plant, different, a peony not a rose was planted and her front porch expanded and grew, made with new wood and the plant blossomed.*

Now Eve stopped and looked at the thorny stick that stood at the front of her house, testifying to the end of so much she had cherished. *"You know you need to dig that up."* The words resounded through her soul. Without saying a word, she accepted the finality of God's iron will and picked up her spade and dug up the dead bush.

Dirt puffed in her face, it was hot and dry. She worked and cried. She wanted to rant and scream at Him. She wanted to call Him names, what He had done to her was unthinkable, but her heart was stilled and resolved within her. His compassion in giving her those early years of bliss with Josiah overwhelmed her, as did her knowledge that her present pain was not enough to make her regret any of the joy she had known. Tears filled her eyes. Eve grieved. Not only for the loss of her love and friend, but for her own dreams. She had in her youth fostered her own hopes for the future, her own day dreams of growing old with Josiah, of a life here in this place, watching their children grow. Glancing at the sky she realized they were both still going to watch the same days unfold, they were now simply separated to different sections of the grand theatre. She was here, low in the main level, while he had been promoted to a booth high above. She cursed the day her own heart had dared to lift its face and try to perceive the path before her, clearly now she was all too aware that God alone directed her steps, and He had in no way broken any promise He had ever made to her. She was not alone, He was with her, her children were with her, and she had been partnered in a marriage contract with Josiah until death parted them. Her own dreams of happily ever after shamed her now in the face of the cruel reality that is the pain of truly loving another person; corruptible and mortal as they are.

As Eve covered the ground where the flower had been, she also buried all her faded hopes and dreams and asked God to give her the strength to press on toward the promises He had dared to whisper to her heart.

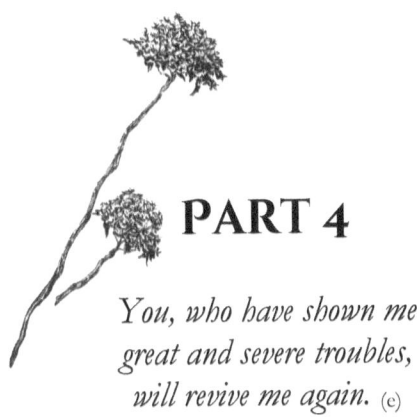

PART 4

*You, who have shown me
great and severe troubles,
will revive me again.* (c)

It once had shone so bright and clear
The promise of this new Frontier
Yet over time the gleam can fade
As we settle for a darker shade
But love and hope are ever true
And we are blessed with visions, new.

"Hey, Mr. Bates!" his foreman yelled. John turned his gaze from the lovely wilderness and saw Parker weaving his way toward him through the construction camp.

At the sound of Mr. Bates' name being called, a man, dressed in fine black western clothes turned. He was wealthy and despite the fact that he was no one in particular here, his money and influence in his little part of the world had allowed him to retain an air of self- importance which gave him no scruples about interrupting the engineer's journey to the 23rd piling.

"Well hey, Mister Bates!" He boomed and catching the Englishman's attention, he stepped forward with a firm handshake. "My name is Trevor Stanton, and you must be the famous John Bates." Bates took the hand and eyed the man with an amused interest, taking in the cut of his suit and shiny silver buttons. The man must have traveled from the West. "I am I take it you're not from around here either." Trevor nodded with pride, "No, no I'm not. I can see we are both men, far from home, fit to work on the great dream that is

57

America. But, I can see you're a busy man," he said pointing to the nearly completely bridge behind Bates, "So I'll only take a minute of your time. I'm looking to enlist your valuable services, and I'd like to take you out to dinner tonight, if that'd be alright, to discuss it."

Bates looked around; it would be difficult for him to break away today, even for the evening meal. "Well, dinner comes and goes around here without much notice on a day like today, would tomorrow suit?" Stanton raised his hand for another enthusiastic handshake, "Tomorrow it is. How's the diner in town at six?" Bates nodded, "I'll see you there." Stanton's smile beamed and he turned and sauntered off. But Bates stood for a moment and watched with curiosity as the man walked off, for he had a strange feeling. For some reason he instantly liked and wanted to trust the man, but something elusive and disconcerting gave him pause.

"Well Mr. Stanton," John was saying over dinner, "It sounds like a very interesting project, however, I couldn't really be sure of anything until I came and looked at it myself." Stanton smiled, "Well, I can tell that you're a man who likes a challenge, Mr. Bates." Mr. Bates smiled slightly, although it was true he was unsure of taking this job, he had a few others offers he was already considering, as the bridge was near completion. Yet, something in him was stirred, and memories he had thought long dormant resurfaced. He had traveled West in his youth with his father and the memories of the place swayed his opinion slightly, but he didn't let Stanton see that.

Stanton could see he didn't have Bates fully on board. Stanton toned down his exuberance and took a very serious tone, "Mr. Bates, I know I could sit here and rattle on about the salary I'm prepared to offer you and the full room and board and the unknown perils of the West to try to seduce you to take what I could paint as an adventurous chapter in your career, but the truth is, my home, my town is in real danger and I've come to you in search of a miracle." Stanton looked around the room, "I've searched long and hard for an engineer and no one comes close to you. What can I say? You're reputation precedes you. But I'm going to need to know, rather quickly, if you are willing to help us, and by us I mean the two hundred men, women, and children who have carved out a good life for themselves in a wild country."

Bates lowered his eyes and ran through some of his thoughts. He finally looked up. "My work here is still two weeks from completion, but give me tonight to think it over and I'll have my answer to you tomorrow."

Mr. Stanton swallowed back a bit of disappointment, "Well, that's fair, I won't pull you from the site another day, I'll come to you to get your answer in the morning if that's all right." Mr. Bates nodded and rising from his chair took Mr. Stanton's hand.

When Bates stepped out of the door into the bright sunlight, his eyes took a moment to adjust. Yet, once they did he realized he was facing west, and his heart was stirred by the vast country that stretched out before him far beyond what his physical sight could perceive.

John wasn't the kind of man who usually knelt to pray, but that night he did. He had traveled to various parts of the world for his work yet no place had ever caused him to take such a pause. It was usual for him to 'go where the job was', but this was different and he couldn't understand why. He felt a strange pull to go west.

It was his desire to go that gave him pause, because he couldn't explain exactly why. When his mind finally stopped turning that night and he drifted off to sleep, he dreamt. *He was moving high above the land, looking down on the countryside. He was so high that when he turned his gaze he could easily perceive the continent of Europe and his home. Once he was aware that he could go there if he chose, he felt free to turn his gaze west again. This time the land moved quickly underneath him, images of the vast mountain ranges, divided by rivers and valleys whizzed past him and soon slowed over a small and unremarkable town nestled at the foot of a mountainside.*

A voice boomed overhead, "You won't be able to fix it." was followed by or within a sound like a rumble of thunder and water began to pour over everything. There was a great flood and John found himself standing on the edge of a wooded area, looking across a flooded river. He heard the sound of people crying but it had grown dark and he couldn't see across the water, but their cries continued. A voice loud and familiar permeated his soul, "Build a bridge." He looked around, he had nothing, no materials; there wasn't even a fallen log that could possibly span the distance that was required. He had nothing and felt the cold pang of desperation clamp around his heart, when he heard them cry out again. Understanding washed over him and the darkness released its hold of him as hope pushed its way through. The voices, they could get across the water, and as he realized that he couldn't 'build' a bridge out of wood or stone, he could build a way to them with his voice. The cries rose in volume as the water began to surge at a greater velocity; he called out and his voice echoed across the water, "Hold on, I am coming!"

He woke slowly, feeling as if he was coming to the surface for air after being underwater for a long time. When he finally broke from his dream state into wakefulness, he couldn't remember what he had dreamt. But his heart was full of deep care and concern that felt like a load of bricks had been placed on his chest while he slept. He sat up and rubbing his face stood and moved toward the wash basin.

He was still groggy and tipped the pitcher too quickly. Water poured out and splashed into and out of the basin. The realization caused him to start and yank the pitcher up. He knocked the bottom of the jug into the basin and sent it crashing to the floor. The terrible sound of the dish shattering jolted him and his dream flooded the foreground of his mind; the terrible sound and the flood waters and the darkness. And the voice, like in the dream filled his head again, faint this time, barely a whisper that was hardly able to rise above his own thoughts, and yet it did. *'You won't be able to fix it.'* The solitary contemplation of his internal revelation began to waver as he heard someone speaking to him. Turning toward the sound he saw his foreman standing at the door of his tent, looking in, drawn to check on John by the sound of the crash. John blinked at the realization of his presence, and found that he hadn't been able to catch what had been said. "What was that?" He asked. His foreman pointed to the broken dish at his feet, "I said, you won't be able to fix it." And seeing that John was fine and there was no need of him he turned and walked away, leaving the tent flap open and the golden light of a new dawn shining in around John Bates as he realized all he could do was pick up the broken pieces.

Your hope is false, your eyes can't see,
that letting go, is now the key.
For silver sheen, you long have fought,
but without a spirit, the body rots.

The coach rolled into town in a cloud of dust, and Mr. Trevor Stanton was there to greet Mr. Bates personally. "Well, hello, hello, Mr. Bates. It is good to see you again." He said in his usually charming way. "Let me have my man get your bags for you." Mr. Stanton turned and bellowed, "Tommy! Get Mr. Bates' things." The young man standing beside him moved forward and began wrestling a trunk off the stage. One very large trunk was all the coachmen turned over and Mr. Stanton looked a bit surprised. "Is this all you've brought?" Mr. Bates nodded, "I've grown accustomed to life on the road. But there is one more which contains my equipment." Mr. Stanton nodded to Tommy who ran around the coach and found the other trunk, "I like that," Mr. Stanton went on, "a self-sufficient man. We are all we need, am I right?" Mr. Bates had to smile at Mr. Stanton's inability to realize how ridiculous he sounded at times. Mr. Stanton clapped his hands in earnest expectation, "Well, I know you've had a long journey, and I completely understand if you're not up to a tour just yet..." Mr. Bates glanced around. "Actually, I'd like to stretch my legs." He said and glanced at his trunks. Mr. Stanton seemed to have everything prepared, "Don't you worry, I'll have my man bring it over to where you'll be staying and we'll end the tour there in a bit. Does that sound alright to you?" Mr. Bates nodded.

Mr. Stanton swung his arms wide as they turned out into the dirty street. "I know you are a man of the world Mr. Bates, but let me assure you our little town is lacking nothing when it comes to our hospitality. My hope is that your wandering heart may even fall in love with our little piece of heaven and join those who have come before you to settle this great land." He smiled and strolled on, Mr. Bates was happy to remain silent and let Mr. Stanton revel in his paternal pride of the little town he had worked so hard to build.

They walked on past the General Store, the Post Office, the Stanton Hotel, numerous saloon's which were topped with second stories where ladies clothed in risqué fashions dared to wave to Mr. Stanton and his guest. "If you choose, you can want for nothing here." Mr. Bates eyed the rest of the town warily. It wasn't exactly what he had expected. Frontier was a mining town built around the wealth and work that was provided from a rich strain of silver that had been found in the mountain.

The buildings became smaller and more rustic as the road ran on into the distance down the valley the town seemed to be nestled in. Mr. Stanton stopped here and grew serious; pointing down the road he said, "Two miles down the valley is the entrance to the mine and another five miles past that is the dam. I'll take you out there tomorrow, let you have a look around, and see what might be done. The river seems to be growing and our humble beginnings aren't going to be enough to hold it back." He looked at Mr. Bates, "I want to thank you for coming all this way to help me out, Mr. Bates." John studied his host with concerned interest, "You know, I may not be able to do anything. I won't know until…" Mr. Stanton interrupted him, "I know, don't put the cart before the horse, so to speak. Well," he said, turning and pointing toward a two story house behind them, "This is Miss Ruth's; she runs this little boarding house, which is where you'll be staying. Now she may not be what you expected to find out here, but let me assure you, you won't find better food anywhere." He turned and led the way.

Three good raps on the door brought a large black woman to open it. Mr. Bates was pleasantly surprised to see Mr. Stanton tip his hat to her, "Well, good evening Miss Ruth, I have brought you an Englishman for supper." Miss Ruth burst out laughing, "You watch yourself, Mr. Stanton, poor man likely to think I'm gonna fry him up for dinner." Mr. Stanton smiled and introduced Mr. Bates, only to have Miss Ruth wave the formalities off. "Don't no one in this town not know 'bout the man you've brought here to save your mine, Mr. Stanton." Mr. Bates glanced at Mr. Stanton, at this new thought, *save the mine?* But Mr. Stanton seemed unaware as he smiled at Miss Ruth's antics. "Now, you'll be staying for dinner, too, Mr. Stanton." It was more of a command than a question and Mr. Stanton agreed. Miss Ruth turned and led the way into the house, shaking her head and talking more to herself, "Poor man been traveling for weeks, thin as a rail he is, we'll get him some real food, yes, we will. O Lord bless him."

The next morning Mr. Bates discovered that Stanton had hired Tommy to be Mr. Bates guide and general errand boy for his entire stay. He was a solid country boy without much book learning, but a good attitude and an enthusiasm for working with the 'engineer' that soon endeared him to John. The first thing Mr. Bates asked of Tommy was to take him on a hike to a vantage that allowed a good view of the valley and dam. Tommy seemed a bit surprised that Mr. Bates didn't want to go directly to the dam itself first, but John explained it helped to get a bird's eye view first, and soon they were on their way up above the town.

At dinner the night before he had been informed that Mr. Stanton was prepared to turn over a good number of his workers in the mine to be laborers in the repairs on the dam, or whatever Mr. Bates might deem necessary. Mr. Stanton's 'fix it' attitude was alarming to say the least. Mr. Bates didn't yet know how to explain, that dams were not usually, fixable.

Tommy was rattling on as they walked up the trail. "So there my daddy stood, wearing my mother's house coat, with his rifle in one hand and that darn coon in the other. One shot, right through the head. I told him that he should try wearing mom's robe when we go deer hunting, since it obviously improved his aim. So I took the rascal, the coon, not my daddy, out on the back parcel and buried it, but you know what, our dog kept digging it up. Every morning we'd wake up and find the nasty thing in the yard again. Finally, I covered the grave with rocks and peed all around it, well, I figured, I needed to speak in a language the dog would understand, and you know what, he never touched it again." Tommy had stopped and turned. "Well, we're just about there Mr. Bates, it's just around the bend there." Bates looked up, he could no longer see a ridge line through the trees. "Oh, very good, shall we keep going?" Tommy smiled, "Well, I sure wouldn't take you for a city fella, Mr. Bates. You know my sister almost ran away with a city fella once…" Bates walked on ahead this time while Tommy carried on with another amusing story.

The trees ebbed away before them and John Bates found himself standing in a grassy meadow that had an expansive view of the valley below. They walked to the edge and Tommy nodded, "This here's the best view but there are some other places if you want a closer look at the mine or the dam."

Mr. Bate had taken out a notebook and was jotting a few things down. The mention of the mine again stirred his curiosity. "Tommy, what is the relationship between the mine and the dam exactly?" Tommy looked at him, surprised by the question, "I thought Mr. Stanton would have told you all about it by now." Mr. Bates nodded, "he's told me a bit, but I'd like to know what you think about it all. Have you worked in the mine?"

Tommy seemed to grow a bit tense and seemed almost nervous. He shifted his gaze back out over the valley and shoved his hands in his pockets. He glanced at Mr. Bates and seemed to make up his mind about something and sighed. "Mr. Bates, I need you to know that I hold Mr. Stanton in very high regard and I don't in any way mean to disrespect him." Mr. Bates was intent, "Yes, Tommy, I understand." Tommy looked down, "Well, sir, it's just that a couple years ago, there was a terrible accident in one of the shafts. And well, the place flooded and some miners were killed. Mr. Stanton hasn't been able to get production back up since then." Tommy broke the small stick he was playing with and threw it. "Look, I don't know much about building things much bigger than a tool shed, but I think the mining has chiseled away into the mountain and it's not necessarily the dam, but the mountain that's gonna break." Tommy looked Bates straight in the eye, "You should know I'm working for you because most of us would rather do anything than go back into those tunnels, we all know it's only a matter of time."

Mr. Bates looked down upon the town. The majority of the buildings and houses were built upon the green plains that ran alongside the small river. Bates scanned the path of the flow. The dam was large, larger than he would have expected. He guessed the rich resource of a silver mine had aided in the building costs. Mr. Bates was irritated. Stanton had drastically understated his priorities as far as the mine was concerned. "Tommy, can you take me to the mine's foreman? I'd like to talk to him."

When they turned to head back down the mountain they were both surprised to see a Native man standing just in front of the tree line, quietly observing them. Mr. Bates looked to Tommy who seemed to only be surprised for a moment and then begin yelling at the Native. "Oh, hell Blue, you just about scared me to death. You know better than to sneak up on me like that." The man laughed as he stepped toward them, "And I thought I taught a young boy named Tommy Jackson that he needed to talk less and listen more if he was to walk in the woods unnoticed." Tommy gave a silent admission as he bowed his head and clenched his jaws. "Mr. Bates this is one of our Native neighbors, Blue Cloud, Blue Cloud this is Mr. John Bates." The two men shook hands and Mr. Bates felt a bit unnerved by the steady and unmoving gaze of the others dark brown eyes. He somehow got the feeling that this man was inspecting him.

Tommy seemed to feel the need to talk. "Mr. Bates here has been hired to try to fix the dam."

Blue Cloud made a soft hmmmm sound as if taking this in while he assessed Mr. Bates. Blue Cloud turned his gaze out toward the valley and spoke as if to no one in particular and yet as if he was talking to everything, even the rocks, "Just like a grieving woman cannot hold back her tears, so the dam will not be able to hold the river back anymore. There are some horses that are never meant to be tamed by man, but were made with a heart that will only follow the breath of the Creator across the prairie, so the river is going to break out of its harness and run as it's Maker calls it to."

Tommy shook his head and turned away, he knew Blue Cloud could go off the deep end at times, but this was pushing it.

Mr. Bates looked intently at the man, his words made sense, in a strange way. Mr. Bates had seen enough of the area in his few days here to be able to say that he would not have designed and placed a dam in that particular location. It made sense, for a season, but now the dam seemed to simply be in the wrong place, for it was a different time now. Mr. Bates lifted his gaze around to the vista below and asked, "How long have your people lived along this river?" When he turned his gaze back to Blue Cloud he found a pleased look of acceptance had wrapped itself around the dark eyes of the Indian. "Ours is a long story Mr. Bates."

PART 5

There was a man sent from God,
whose name was John. (f)

The tinkle of crystal,
the shatter of glass
A glimmer of hope,
how long will it last?

The cool night was kept at bay by the warm glow of many lamps and crackling fires. Mr. Stanton had arranged a formal dinner for his new found hope, Mr. Bates. Mr. Stanton was comfortable and proud of his wealth, and the friends that it attracted. Mr. Bates was a reserved observer and found the company and conversation provided an interesting mixture of information and amusement.

Mr. and Mrs. Brown were the least among the wealthy in the little town, so that is to say that Mr. Bates liked them the most out of the party. They owned a small shipping company and ran the General Store and although they had prospered in the shadow of the mine, they were a rustic, down to earth sort who hoped to be influential in the shaping of the wilderness into civilization. Their two sons were grown and starting families of their own, giving the Browns' a healthy interest in the development of the school system.

"Of course, we've come a long way from the little school the missionaries started for the natives, but we still have a long way to go." Mrs. Brown was saying to a Miss Swanson, the local school teacher. Miss Swanson steeled herself against the remark, "Yes, well I do my best I'm sure." She replied, though her eyes were on Mr. Bates. He gave her a slight smile and turned his gaze back to Mr. Brown who was speaking with Mr. Stanton. But Miss Swanson, who was pretty and young, had been moved West by her ambitious father and was resolved to teach only as a way to pass the time until she could be married. And so she turned her attention toward engaging the conversation of the handsome engineer rather than continue the more academic conversation with her neighbor. "How long do you think you will be in the area, Mr. Bates? Will it take long for you to get the mine up and running again?" Mr. Bates lowered his eyes; again he was irritated by the reference to the repairing of the mine rather than the dam. "Well, I don't know much about the running of mine's. My primary focus is on the integrity of the dam and whether or not anything can be done about it at this point." He stated, matter-of-factly. This caused a sudden hush to fall around the dinner table and Mr. Stanton's eyes glinted as he swirled the wine in his glass. "Well," he said drawing into the conversation, "The mine is so close to the dam, there really is no separating of the two. Their destinies, like so many of ours, are intertwined, am I right Mr. Bates?"

Mr. Bates looked long and hard at his host. He was being put in a very awkward position, one that he would never have chosen for himself. Miss Swanson chimed in again, before he could fully collect his thoughts on the matter. "Is there a very great danger of the dam failing?" She said with almost a childlike ignorance that surprised Mr. Bates. He tried to answer in the most diplomatic way possible. "I haven't had enough time yet to gather the needed information about the river and the original building of the dam to be certain of anything at this point." Mr. Conolly, a rotund man who was seated beside Mr. Stanton posed the next question, "And how will you go about discovering such histories? I'm sure no one here remembers when the dam was built. That was well over sixty-five years ago now." Mr. Bates calmed himself, this train of conversation no longer grating on his nerves, but it was Stanton who answered the question, "I have the original plans of the dam, and a few other documents that my grandfather had tucked away, all ready for your perusal Mr. Bates." He said and nodded as if he alone was capable of bestowing such a gift.

Mr. Bates was now so fully irritated by the man that he volunteered, "I have also met one of the natives and I plan to eventually meet with the elders and learn what I can of the river's history from them." All eyes turned toward him in shocked silence. Mr. Bates had effectively tested and proven the racial prejudice of the room. Mr. Stanton looked into his wine glass as he swirled it again, his mouth pursing as if he held something sour on his tongue. Finally, he clapped his hands and leaned forward, "Well, Mr. Bates, I hope that you discover all you need to know about our river, but for now I think that's enough talk of business." He looked around the table, "This is supposed to be a dinner *party*, am I right?" and with his usual engaging manner asked, "Shall we all move into the front room?" Everyone seemed to be eager to move and change the uncomfortable atmosphere.

Mr. Bates woke the next morning disheartened by the way the evening had gone. He wished to think well of Mr. Stanton and his friends, and yet, there was something very troubling about their attitude in the town's present situation. So he set himself toward the task ahead of him, inspecting the dam, mine, and river while trying to be unmoved by the current prejudices and expectations.

Mr. Bates made his way down the stairs into the sunlit kitchen where Miss Ruth was fixing a pot of tea for him. She only had one other boarder and Mr. Bates had heard him come in rather late in the night.

Miss Ruth turned and saw him standing in the doorway. "Well, my, my you's looking all sorts of frazzled this morning, Mr. Bates." Bates lifted his hand up to his hair, and Miss Ruth smiled at him as she set breakfast things onto the table. "You look just fine, Mr. Bates, but it's showing in your eyes now. You're not sure about why you're here, are you?" She motioned to the chair at the table. Mr. Bates leaned forward and wrapped his hands around his mug. He liked Miss Ruth and felt he could trust her. "No, I'm not. I thought Mr. Stanton was, well, I thought he had brought me here to help save the town, but now I fear…." Miss Ruth was stirring a large pot on the stove and waved her hand at him, then turned and crossed the room to join him at the table while she spoke, "Oh, Mr. Bates, anyone could have told you that man cares more for that mine than he does the poor folks of this community. Everyone, that is but Mr. Stanton himself. Lord, bless him, but he thinks he made this town, his family anyway, but that ain't the truth of it." Mr. Bates was interested in the history, "Who founded the town then?" Miss Ruth rocked back a bit in her chair as she went on, "Why, that depends on how you define 'founded' and what you mean by 'town' doesn't it? " She chuckled, "Some people, like the Stanton's think they own that river because they've been able to hold it back for so long, but the Indians were here first, and even before they were here, it was God who done made that river, so who do you think really owns this place Mr. Bates?" Bates was smiling to himself, he liked Ruth. Yet, he did not hold Mr. Stanton's concerns for the mine against him, simply the fact that he had been deceptive about it. Miss Ruth shifted in her chair and went on as she let her eyes drift out the window and up to the hills and trees then she said, "The Indians were here first, they lived in this valley for hundreds of years and the first white men they saw were the missionaries. Those missionaries are the ones who started the town. They built the first church and school and they lived in peace here, that is, until more white men came and silver was found in the mountain." Miss Ruth sighed, the sunlight was framing her face in a way that made her look ancient and enchanted. Mr. Bates was caught in the moment, mesmerized as she continued, "Then came all sorts of troubles and sadness. Fighting and wars. The Indians were finally pushed back to the other side of the mountain and the dam made so that the mine could be built nearest the largest veins of silver." Mr. Bates was gazing off into space at the moment, taking the history of the place in and wondering what he could do. The roots of the problem ran deep, generations deep, and the fixing of a dam wouldn't be enough to bring this town into the bright future that could be possible for it.

Miss Ruth had turned her face toward him and was observing him with some interest. "I suspect, Mr. Bates, that God didn't bring you here to fix that dam. And if that be the case, then what you need to find out is why He done brought you here." Mr. Bates sat up and his brow furrowed slightly. He still had some searching out to do before he came to his final decision about the dam. He intended to meet with some of the miners and discover the truth about the flooding and what the actual problems were, and he was engaged to spend some time with the Indians and discover what he could about the size and flow of the river as far back as they could tell him. Mr. Bates was unaware of the peculiar look Miss Ruth was giving him and was only shaken from his thoughts by a rap at the door. Miss Ruth heard it as well and wiggled her jolly rolls out of her chair and moved for the door. Mr. Bates went back to his breakfast and was nearly sunk back into deep thought when the visitor was let in.

"Good morning Miss Ruth. Oh, did you forget? You asked me to come and hang that bedroom door." Miss Ruth laughed, "Sweet Jesus, thank you Lee. No I ain't forgot, I just got caught up in other things and forgot it was to be today. Just you this morning?" She said letting the man in the door, Mr. Bates could hear the respectful stomping off of boots before the other stepped into the house. "Oh no, Eve came out with me to visit with you while I worked, if that's alright. She's out seeing to the horses now." Miss Ruth stepped back into the kitchen doorway, "Well come in and meet my new guest." She was saying and Mr. Bates turned from his breakfast to meet Miss Ruth's friend. Miss Ruth made the introductions, "Mr. Bates, this is our Pastor, Mr. Lee Wood. Lee this here's the engineer Mr. Stanton brought in, Mr. Bates."

Mr. Wood wore plain western clothing, a plaid shirt with a vest, which held a watch in the pocket, evidenced by the silver chain that scrolled across his belly. His hair was thinning and his beard was speckled with grey, but his eyes were open and bright and he set down his tool box and extended a large strong hand to the visitor. "It's nice to meet you Mr. Bates." He said with a winning smile, Mr. Bates liked the man immediately. "And you Mr. Wood." Miss Ruth explained, "Lee here's a master carpenter and I'd hoped to get the third bedroom's door back on its hinges, and perhaps oil the hinges on the others, they've been squeakin' something fierce." Mr. Wood was smiling at Miss Ruth as if he suspected fully that the squeaking of the door wouldn't be so bothersome if the man renting the room didn't let it swing at two in the morning.

"Well, Mr. Wood," Mr. Bates started, but was stopped. The pastor raised a hand, "Please, Lee will do just fine." Mr. Bates smiled, "Very well, then I think John will do as well. Could you use a hand with anything? I've nothing pressing to get to this morning." Lee nodded, "Actually, I could use an extra set of hands, I've got to frame in the doorway and then set the door." It was settled and the two of them went up the stair with Miss Ruth calling after them, "Lee, ol Harvey mo'n likely has a sore head this morning, stumbling in here late last night, so don't spare that hammer, none!" Mr. Bates and Lee chuckled as they turned the corner up the stairs. Miss Ruth was willing to make a ruckus in order to restore peace to her nights.

Miss Ruth went back into the kitchen and so it was that Mr. Bates came down the stairs in search of the hammer when Eve came in the door.

Eve was looking down and talking, thinking it was Miss Ruth who was in the room with her. Her arms were full of Christmas ribbons and a set of brass candlesticks and other items which were trying to escape her grasp. "I've brought your decorations back from the chapel...my box broke..." she was saying as she picked up a tangle of string and ribbon and turning she caught sight of Mr. Bates. At the appearance of him, standing there so calmly and naturally, one of the candlesticks fell from her hand and sounded a chime as it hit the floor and rolled toward him. The sound should have brought her to her senses but she seemed quite taken away, as if the slowly rolling object was pulling her along with it to another place.

Eve stood and watched as it stopped against the toe of his boot. He picked up the candle stick and moved to hand it to her. His face was momentarily brushed with a puzzled look. Eve shook her head slightly not trusting her voice just yet. She reached out to take the candlestick. His fingers touched hers so quickly the contact was broken before she realized it had happened. "Miss Ruth loaned these things to the church for the holidays but we're done with them now." Her words felt hollow and dumb, mundane speech that could in no way portray all she was feeling, much to her relief. She stood then, with her arms over flowing with the discarded Christmas season, unruly strands of hair falling around her flustered expression and Mr. Bates had to force his eyes away from hers.

Miss Ruth appeared and opened the closet and let Eve empty her arms. Eve laughed as Miss Ruth was now free to give her friend a 'hello' hug, but made it a quick embrace, and taking Eve's hand turned her around to properly introduce her to Mr. Bates. "Mr. Bates, this is my dear friend, Mrs. Eve Carson, Mr. Lee's daughter. Eve, this here's Mr. Bates, all the way from England." Mr. Bates tried not to show his surprising disappointment at the introduction which had bestowed a Mrs. Carson on whom he had hoped was still a Miss Wood.

Mr. Bates then seemed to remember that he had something to do. "Miss Ruth, Lee sent me down in search of another hammer." Miss Ruth nodded, "Well sure, Mr. Bates," she said, reaching into the open closet behind her and producing the item. Mr. Bates took it and giving a little salute with it said, "Well, it was nice to meet you, but I'd best get back up there." The sound of her father's hammer seemed to shake the house. Eve simply nodded and watched him walk back up the stairs. She turned and saw Miss Ruth posed with one of her, 'well my, my, what do you think of that' looks that

Eve knew only too well. Eve tried to ignore it as she turned into the kitchen for a cup of tea. Miss Ruth simply shook her head and laughed as she spoke softly, "All right Lord, I can see we's gotta a little work to do here."

The work on the new door took a few hours, and by that time Miss Ruth had decided Lee and Eve needed to stay on for lunch before taking their cold drive home. Lee and John were soon seated at the table enjoying each other's company while Eve and Miss Ruth prepared the food. Lee put down his cup and leaned forward, "So, John, what exactly is going on here, with you and the dam project?" John set his cup down. "Well, I can only tell you what I've been telling everyone, I simply don't know just yet." Lee seemed to have many thoughts on the matter, "Have you been out to the village yet?" Mr. Bates shook his head, "No, not yet, I met a man named Blue Cloud, he's planning to take me out day after tomorrow." Lee nodded, "Well, you should also talk to Brian Cuthright. He was the mining foreman until…" he glanced at his daughter who seemed busy and unaware of what was being said at the moment, "the flooding began in the shafts." Mr. Bates found this interesting, "Where can I find him?" Lee answered, "Well, he lives outside of town up on the mountain, trying to prospect his own strain now, but I could take you up there, if you'd like." Mr. Bates like the sound of that, still Lee was hoping to understand a little more.

"So, do you think the dam will break?" Lee asked. Mr. Bates didn't want to start unnecessary panic, but he felt confident that Lee had a good head and real desire for the truth. "It's hard to say. Considering the location of the dam and the mine and the size of the river, I think it could be a very likely possibility. It's rare to get a warning, most dams burst without one. I'm amazed that the initial breaches in the mine were so long ago, actually. It seems unlikely to me that those collapses in any way have contributed to a degradation of the dam's integrity, in truth, if they had, the dam would have collapsed long ago. I'm having a bit of trouble understanding the cause of the present concern for the sake of the dam." Lee clasped his hands between his knees and glanced at his daughter again. "We have a bit of an interesting perspective on that and it's a little hard to explain. Why don't we talk about that another time?"

Eve hadn't been paying too much attention, but at that moment, Mr. Bates spoke, and something about his voice and manner of speaking, when paired with what he said, broke through her present thought process, "Well, it is an interesting thought, for the dam isn't necessarily that old, and the truth is it can be better to let go and have a new start of things. But that's not exactly an easy thing to do for most people, especially an entire town."

The idea of the dam actually bursting and flooding the town that filled the basin held Mr. Bates in the moment. His dream and the broken basin were brought to mind and he gazed absentmindedly at Eve while she cleaned up the dishes and tried not to notice him. He was caught by the understanding that he was to care more about the people here who were like Eve, than he was to care about the dam.

Eve was putting on her coat. She had a moment alone in the hallway and was glad no one could see how her fingers were fumbling with the buttons. Mr. Bates stepped into the hall. He had had a very enjoyable morning with Lee and wanted to pay his respects to his daughter. "It was very nice to meet you," he said, and Eve was relieved that he didn't extend his hand toward her. "Perhaps next time I'll be able to meet the rest of your family." Eve felt a bit flustered by the comment, "Yes, I suppose." Lee came down the stairs with his tool box in one hand and a knowing glance passing over the top of his glasses to his daughter. She drew back a bit, embarrassed by what her father was obviously thinking, but he turned toward Mr. Bates. "Yes, John, I'll talk to the wife and we'll have you over soon. " He glanced at his daughter and went on, "Yeah, little Samuel is what nine, now Eve, and the other two are in line a year each above him." Mr. Bates raised his eyebrows at this information. "Well, I'd be pleased to meet them and their father too no doubt," he said with a nod back to Eve. Eve smiled slightly, as was polite but found herself unable to speak the very thing she desired to say. "My husband is dead." The words filled her belly and rose up her throat but she choked on them and it was all she could do to stand there and not burst into tears. She was surprised by the feelings this man was stirring within her. She wanted to be free from the meeting at once. Loyalty to Josiah flooded her and despite all she had gone through she felt nagged by thoughts that she was in some way being unfaithful to him.

Mr. Bates looked at her with wonder, unable to understand why her presence was affecting him so. Thankfully Miss Ruth entered the room and wrapped an arm around Eve's shoulder. But before Miss Ruth could say anything, Eve turned into her arms and hugged her good-bye, abruptly ending the discussion of her marital status while avoiding noticing how Mr. Bates had responded to Miss Ruth's intrusion to their conversation. He felt saddened that is was over so suddenly. Eve wanted to get away and said, "Thank you for lunch." then turning she added, "And it was very nice to meet you Mr. Bates," she nodded to her father before quickly ducking out the door. Lee said his good-byes as well, giving John a firm handshake and every assurance that he would be by later in the week to take him to meet Brian and have him over to the house for dinner.

Out on the front porch, Eve thanked God for the frigid air that cooled the flush that had risen to her cheeks so unexpectedly. She felt all jumbled up and out of sorts as she headed to the wagon.

She sat quietly as her father climbed in a moment later beside her. "Well, Evie, what do you think of that Mr. Bates?" He was smiling as he gathered the reins. Eve turned toward him, "Yes, he seems like a good sort of man." and she hoped that would be an end of the conversation, for being free of the man's presence had not cooled the many sensations seeing him had caused within her. She looked back at the house and wondered at the whole thing. There was a strangeness coupled with a familiarity about him that unnerved her to the core. A part of her was screaming for joy while the rest of her seemed locked in a mud pit of stark reality and present sensibility. When her dad spoke again, Eve was confronted by how little he seemed to know of what she was going through. "Perhaps the town has a chance after all…" he was saying and went on talking about the dam and mine. Eve listened and tried to set her thoughts on that situation and was actually irritated to find that it was hard for her to do so.

Eve looked back at Ruth's house as they drove off. A strange feeling still lingered and try as she may she could not shake it. She was irritated by the entire encounter. A part of her knew exactly who Mr. Bates was to her, but again God was doing things in His timing not hers, she was not ready for this and resolved to have a long talk with God about it later, until then she would adopt an attitude of pure denial.

PART 6

Behold,
the former things have come to pass,
And new things do I declare;
Before they spring forth I tell you of them. (g)

Can it be that what I see,
is what you showed me long ago?
I've wrestled on with doubts and fears, struggled
against what I know.
Now I see a ray of hope,
and love has bent his bow.
Do I have the strength to walk,
the path you dared to show?

Water trickled down stone in the walls of the mine. Mr. Bates had spent well over a month, going over the mines original plans and inspecting every aspect of the dam he could think of. He had continued in a good friendship with Lee and had made a habit of visiting out at his place at least once a week, if not more. Today he stood looking up at the tall gray wall that was holding back a river and he felt frustrated. He could find no evidence that the dam had lost any integrity. There was no reason for him to believe that with proper maintenance and the building of a few reinforcements the dam wouldn't continue on as it was for some time. Yet, he did have a nagging sense that there was still something he couldn't see, something he hadn't yet accounted for and he was determined to turn over every stone until he was satisfied.

He heard his name and turning saw Tommy coming toward him. "Well, perhaps the Natives would be able to tell him something." he thought to himself. He decided to ask Blue Cloud to finally take him out to visit his people.

Eve wasn't aware of the faint smile that was daring to cling to the corner of her mouth. Bathed in sunlight she was enjoying the musical tones of the dishwater. Far away down the hall were many sounds of children clamoring around the house. Alone in the kitchen she found her heart made glad, but she tried to retreat back into a shadow of doubt as she realized what had caused her to hope. She set the dish she was working on in the drying rack and was determined not to think of Mr. Bates. But she found her head filled with the sound of his voice, and placing her hands on the sides of the sink she stopped her work and took a moment to pause in her task.

The sunlight shone soft and yellow through the pane of glass. The thin lace curtains fluttered in the soft breeze and begged a dance from a few lofty bubbles. Eve was caught by the beauty of the glowing orbs as they twirled before her, the light illuminating a halo of color upon their spherical bodies. The image pierced her soul and memories that resided in the deep places of her spirit surfaced as the present experience glimmered like a light upon the waters of her heart. Eve had seen such things before. She had seen similar forms, and been pulled into them, into another place, into a dream state. At other times she had faint memories of being pulled out of such balls of light just before waking. She let herself wander into thoughts and questions about such things as she lifted a handful of suds and examined the way the colors were changed by the straight angles that were formed when many were gathered together. She blew softly and watched a parade of rainbow painted spheres march out her window upon the wind. In doing so she realized she had sent a bit of the atmosphere from within her house, out into the vast wilderness, wrapped in an envelope of cleansing soap water. She sighed, isn't that just what her dreams were? A breath of heaven wrapped in a palace of ethereal truth that brushed against the doubt and fear she fostered in her heart, every dream an attempt to cleanse her soul by revealing God's plan to her.

Eve sighed. The mortality of her marriage burst many such bubbles, releasing heavens breath into the reality of her life. And it changed everything, she was now constantly aware that God was with her, that He was orchestrating His plans through the rhythm that was her life.

And now she looked at the suds that still clung to the edges of her wash bin, and realized her heart was in a similar state. Although so much had happened, there still remained promises, some sent to her in dreams and through spirit, that hadn't, as yet, been fulfilled. Shiny ethereal hopes were still clinging to the edges of her wounded heart, soothing the ache, without having the power to conquer the pain completely. Eve splashed the water with her fingers and bowed her head and cried an inward prayer. She was tired; she wanted rest, she feared the end of her own strength. How long could promises alone sustain her?

Out the window she could see the last of the bubble train popping, and she was forced to recognize the cold shudder her heart felt at the sight. She was fearful of her dreams coming true and bursting into reality. She had seen it happen terribly before. Yet, even more she feared, despite all that had happened, that her hopes were only dreams, only the cries of her own now lonely heart. But such seeds of doubt found no place to take root in a heart so established after experiencing firsthand the foreknowledge and care of God through the trauma of loss. Now she could look back and see that it was not only the loss of her husband that had wounded her, but loss of her hopes and plans for their life. That was why God had paired her visions of losing Josiah with promises of a hope and future. Now, she found herself waiting for a pleasant coming, and her fear was that she may not have the courage to recognize it when it came.

Eve's eyes could not see that the gentle breeze that at first carried her hopes upon the winds as a simple prayer, continued to flow long after her soap had lost its grip on the air, and the breath of heaven flowed through the nearby woods. The wind called out for her sisters, the Maker stirring the tiny torrent along with His own fingers, encouraging it to grow until a tempest was made of such a force that the trees shook. One lingering pine wobbled as if unclasping its grip from the hand of its mother, the earth, and then not able to stand without support it toppled. It crashed into and knocked down a good portion of fence allowing a herd of cows to pursue greener pastures and dare the unknown.

A call rang out for Eve to go say good-bye to her children for the day, as her parents were driving them into school this morning, and she found that she could not brush the spheres of promise that were quivering in her heart away as easily as the bubbles from her hands.

The front door banged loudly and Eve was called back to the land of the living by her father's strong voice. Eve went through the kitchen doorway and met him in the hall. "What is it?" Eve asked. Her father was shaking the cold morning from his shoulders, and she noticed he wasn't taking his coat off. He answered her quickly, "The north fence is down and I've got twenty head gone. Blue Cloud's here to help me so we're heading out after them, your mothers still fixed to take the kids to school, but I was wondering if you would ride out to the mine. I was supposed to meet Mr. Bates today and take him out to meet Brian Cuthright, but with the weather turning I need to get my cattle in." He seemed upset that he was going to be disrupting Mr. Bates day. "I just don't want to leave him hanging," he continued. "I just need you to give him the message." Eve was thinking it all over, "Well, I could take him out to the camp, Dad, or did you want to take him yourself?" Lee took a minute to process that. "Well, I'd like to be there, but if he's pressed for time, offer to take him today. Tell him I'll be available in two days for sure, perhaps even tomorrow if we find the cows today." Eve nodded, "Alright." and kissing him on the cheek she told him to be careful.

It was a foggy morning and Eve enjoyed the coolness of the air, it seemed to have a soothing effect on her anxiety as she drew closer to mine. The place looked abandoned and she didn't see the horse Mr. Bates usually rode. Instead she saw a creamy gelding and as it turned and looked at her and Raven approach, Eve was shaken with the knowledge that she had seen this horse before, in a dream. The memory flooded her mind and filled her heart with knowledge she felt she could not hold, and yet could not let go of. She steadied herself and pushed the thing out of her mind and looked around. There were men down the hill near the river, mining in the shallow pits there that still produced a bit of silver.

The area looked so bleak and gray. Keeping her hand on her horse for just a moment as she turned her gaze to the main opening of the mine. It stood, black and gaping, like an insatiable mouth. She wondered if she should wait for Mr. Bates to appear or if she should go in looking for him. It seemed silly to wait for what might be hours just to give him a simple message, so steeling herself she lit a lantern from the stack near the arch way and entered the mine.

She wandered through the dark tunnels for only a short time before she was led by the sound of voices. The sound of more than one male voice was reassuring, for some reason she didn't like the thought of Mr. Bates navigating through the mine by himself. Turning a corner Eve caught only a glimpse of Mr. Bates lying on the ground and then Eve thought her lamp went out for everything went black. A dim light broke the darkness and she realized she was looking up and saw a lamp dangling over her, "Billy?" she asked as she saw who it was standing over her, another thump hit her and the light went out again.

Blue Cloud was out in the field forking hay out of the back of the wagon, the thought being the cows may come home at feeding time. Lee was down near the broken fence laying preparations for the repairs, but leaving a large gap open for the cows to come back in through. A great swoosh blew past Blue Cloud and he turned and saw an eagle with a white head rising into the air. A cry rang out and another joined it and the two circled in the sky above him, climbing higher and higher.

Greg Stanley and Billy Jackson were arguing within the mine. "I ain't killing'm Greg! That's Eve Carson in there, she teaches my little sister's Sunday school..." Greg turned and held the spade end of a shovel up to Billy, "We can't let them go, Billy. They saw us, they'll have a posy on us before we get five miles outta here." Greg said. Billy was beside himself, "I… i…I ain't no murderer Greg…I can't do it. Let's just leave'm. They'll be out for a while…" Greg turned and looked behind him, and scratched his beard, "No, there's no telling when they'll wake up…" they finally agreed to chain them and Billy had gently set the light so Mrs. Carson wouldn't wake into the dark. Greg shook his head as Billy walked past him, "Well ain't that sweet, Billy boy." He sneered. Billy walked on shaking his head, this was bad and he was scared. After Billy was well on down the shaft Greg had turned and using his shovel had pried a support beam loose and run off as the rocks tumbled and blocked the way. Billy turned in anger, "What'd ya do that for?" he yelled. Greg turned on him, "You shut-up. I ain't killed 'm just bought us a bit more time. Now come on, we need to get outta here, make us a new start." and with that he slapped Billy on the shoulder and moved on down the mine. Billy looked back with an earnest hopeless expression, but turned and followed Greg out of the tunnel.

Into the dark, into my sleep
I try to run, but promises keep
There is no way to undo time
Or to take away, those things Divine.

Eve woke to the damp smell of water upon stone. She could see faintly and realized her lantern was about five feet from her. At first she thought she must have tripped, but then how would her lamp be sitting perfectly on a piece of lumber so far from her, if that's what happened. A dull aching at the back of her head made its presence known and when she went to reach for it, her right hand felt heavy and dumb. Looking toward it she saw that she was burdened by a heavy chain that had been fastened to her wrist by a lock. This brought her more fully awake and taking hold of it she realized it was well fastened and she could not get her hand out of it. Dropping her hand in her lap she realized she would need something to pick the lock with, she looked around. That was when she saw Mr. Bates laying only a few feet from her, his dark pants blending in perfectly with the rocky floor and the rest of him sprawling out further from the lamp so that she hadn't noticed him.

She was instantly up and kneeling beside him but her bound wrist caught. She saw that the chain was threaded behind a support beam in the wall and the other end of the chain was attached to Mr. Bates' wrist. She couldn't explain how they had gotten in such a situation and after she was satisfied that Mr. Bates was breathing and seemed, as she did, to have only a bump on the head, she tried to wake him.

Eve looked around in desperation. The tunnel leading out of the end of the shaft they were in had been blocked, as if there had been a cave in. Eve wondered if that was what had knocked her out. But how had they been chained? She had no idea what she should do and so turned back to Mr. Bates, his wakefulness becoming her escape from the fearful ranting of her mind. "Mr. Bates!" Nothing. "John, wake up, John. Please!" She looked down at his hand, she wanted so badly to take it, to touch him, shake him, wake him up, but she was held back by an iron grip of morality. The situation accosted all propriety and just when her trembling hand moved his did as well and he groaned as he woke. His hand lifted for his head as he asked her, "What happened?" Eve sat back, hugging her knees, not trusting herself to keep hold of her emotions. Still she managed to say, "I don't know. I came here looking for you and then I woke up here. That's all I know. No, wait, I saw Billy, I remember seeing Billy Jackson." John sat back against the wall and looked around and then he began to piece a few things together. He sounded tired and groggy but he retraced his steps as well, "I sent Tommy back for some tools, and I thought I heard voices. I found...," he sighed and closed his eyes remembering coming men in the mine, "they must have been taking advantage of the mine being shut down. I caught them in the act, stealing ... one of them must have come up behind me with a shovel or something. I don't remember anything else." He stopped talking as he looked around, fully awake now and saw that they were trapped, the shaft caved in. Then looking at Eve, as if noticing her there for the first time, he asked in an irritated tone, "What are you doing here?" Eve didn't care for his paternal tone and retorted, "I came here looking for you. Dad's cows got out and he wasn't going to be able to take you out to Mr. Cuthright's today so he asked me to bring you the message." Mr. Bates eyes fell, such a simple thing, and now look at where they were.

Noticing the lamp he sat up and asked, "Why would they leave us a light? They obviously meant to leave us to die." After he said it he realized it would have been better to not voice such a truth and looked at Eve, but she was looking at the light with a puzzled expression. "I doubt we'll die Mr. Bates, but for some reason they didn't want us to be completely in the dark." she answered. And then looked back down the shaft into the darkness, "I wondered how far that goes, if there's an air shaft or something?" Mr. Bates glanced up, "There's no way to tell from here." Eve stood and took a few steps in that direction, but her arm was chained to Mr. Bates and her movement caused his arm to be pulled across the rocks. She stopped and looked to see that he wasn't hurt and turned toward the light. Even if there was a way out down the tunnel, which seemed unlikely-or if they may be able to dig their way out, they needed to get out of the chains. Mr. Bates was inspecting the lock at his wrist, Eve glanced at him, "How long until you'll be missed?" Mr. Bates looked up at her, "Not until later in the day, I sent Tommy back for my surveying equipment and instructions to meet Lee and I at the mining camp. It could be some time before I'm missed, let alone discovering that we're still in here." Eve nodded, "Same with me, Dad wanted me to give you the message, but if you couldn't wait another day or two he wondered if I might take you to Brian myself. Tommy will wait for a long time before he begins to suspect anything."

Mr. Bates nodded and lifted his head up as if to clear his thoughts. Eve was pacing softly, her agitation growing. The feeling of being trapped was becoming too real. And being chained to Mr. Bates of all people was irritating her greatly. The impropriety of being chained, in this place of perpetual night, to a man who was not her husband raked against her sense of propriety. She clasped and unclasped her hands as loyalty and longing for Josiah threatened to consume her. The sound of the chain clanging slightly as she moved was like a wake- up call she refused to acknowledge.

Mr. Bates tried his belt buckle to pick the lock, but it was no good. Eve did the same with a hair pin, but it proved unfit for the task. John turned to the beam the chain was set around. It would be unwise to move it, it was a support beam, messing with it could bring the place down on them. Still he kept looking for options as Eve grew more restless. She knew someone would come for them, eventually, and yet the idea of being held in such a place was tormenting her. This place made her constantly aware of Josiah's passing. How many times she had seen it happen while she slept? And she found herself wondering if he suffered much, how God may have prepared him for his fate. Still the path of all these wonderings ended at the heavy chain on her wrist and the reality that she was now criminally bound to Mr. Bates.

When she looked over at him, he was sunk down at the bottom of the beam looking up its length then down around the rocks at the base. His presence had a very calming effect on her in many ways, but realizing that only irritated her further.

Looking down at her wrist she fumbled with the chain and rubbed the skin that was red already from the weight of it. A few tears fell from her cheeks as she realized that she could no more break the chain than she could bring Josiah back along with all her lost hopes for her future with him. Mr. Bates, noticing her tears, and misunderstanding them, tried to console her. "It's only a matter of time. They will come looking for us." He said. Looking up at the sudden break of the silence she stood tall and firm, "I'm not afraid of dying, I've been left alone by these tunnels before." She rubbed her wrist again, "Death is not as easy as this. I know we'll live," and with that she sat as if tired of living. Softly she continued, "Just like I know the dam will break."

Mr. Bates looked at Eve. She had laid her head back upon the stone and closed her eyes as if in patient acceptance of all these things. Mr. Bate felt troubled by her words and asked, "How do you 'know' the dam's going to break Eve?" She opened her eyes and looked at him, "Don't you 'know' yet?" she asked. Mr. Bates shook his head, "Dam's break, this is true. But I have found no evidence that persuades me that this dam is beyond hope. I've seen no loss of integrity that other dams haven't lasted through. With continued maintenance and perhaps the rebuilding of a few sections in the future it could very well out last us."

Eve considered this carefully and readjusted herself to look at Mr. Bates better. "But what about what you can't see?" She asked. "What about the other side, the side that's underwater, how do you know what's going on there?" Mr. Bates nodded, "It's true I can't see, but what makes you so sure? Has Stanton had other engineers out here before me?" Eve shook her head, "No, I've just seen the other side, that's all. One day Frontier will be under water."

"How could you possibly know that?"

Eve was stung by his inability to understand her. Her heart was screaming, but her mouth was having trouble finding the words. "I know because…" she started but then had to try again, "I know because…" but Mr. Bates thought she was just being fearful and emotional. Sometimes people, especially women could let their fears run away with them. He interrupted her, "That's just it, you can't *know*, you might feel the valley is unsafe, but you can't know, Eve. No one can."

Now Eve was angry at him. She stood up. She would not suffer his misconceptions. Her knowledge and understanding had cost her dearly. "You have no idea of my feelings or what I know! Not about my home, that dam or…!"Eve stopped herself and changed the direction of her disclosure. "You're so blind! I *know* because the One who knows everything, told me. Just like He's told me…other things that I've seen come true. And the truth is, Mr. Bates that despite all your learning and understanding about dams, God knows more than you and if *He* says it's going to blow, then it will!"

She crumpled to the ground and turned her shoulder away from him as far as the chain would allow. She spoke softly through angry tears that had come. "I hate this, I hate knowing like this. No one else can see, and I hate that and I'm stuck in this dark place…" Eve wanted to add a, 'with you,' to that but found that she couldn't. For some reason she cared for Mr. Bates and did not, now or ever, want to say anything that would cause him harm, although she felt as though perhaps she had. And it really wasn't being here with him that upset her; it was being here at all. It was the fact that this was the path God had designed for her, this *duality*, this having to have a second chance when she was still convinced that her first chance would have been enough. She was feeling things for this man that she didn't want to feel and she was now bound to him. She whispered, "I want to get out. Isn't there some way we can get out of here?"

Mr. Bates could say nothing. He sat looking at her, her face now turned up in the light as she looked around the stony prison. She turned toward him, feeling sorry for her outburst. "Please, forgive me, Mr. Bates. It's not you I'm really angry with." She wiped her forehead. "It's God, I can't escape him. He is love, but sometimes it's a hard love." She noticed a stone sitting beside her, and picking it up she said, "He was the stone I would have rejected but has now become the chief cornerstone of my faith." She dropped it and looked away.

Mr. Bates looked at the stone and in doing so he saw that light was breaking through. It came directly from where the stone had lain. The little ray of light seemed to break through a black curtain and he felt more than he could express to her. "I'm sorry. When Mr. Stanton came for me I was under the impression that the cave in had caused him to fear for the dam...I didn't question." Eve spoke over her shoulder, "That accident didn't cause Stanton to worry...but that was when God dared to ask me to share what I knew with Stanton. If Stanton wanted to he could help the town. He could take steps to move the town to higher ground, away from the danger. The dam breaking is only a change of scenery, it won't be the end, but more could be lost than needs to be, which is why I went to Stanton."

Mr. Bates had grown thoughtful, "But he didn't believe you."

"No, well, he won't admit it anyway." Eve said, "And I have no 'proof' just my repeating what I heard from an invisible God, and I'm not the only one God's talking to, the whole town is anxious about the dam." Eve sighed, "The truth is Stanton has the power to help move the town but he is more interested in his own power and profit than the town as a whole."

Mr. Bates blinked as he realized, "Then there is nothing I can do. There is no way to completely ensure that an apparently sound dam will not burst. You do what you can but there is never a guarantee. A new dam could be built, but in truth it would be better to let the old one go and then rebuild, perhaps farther upstream…" He trailed off his thoughts moving in other directions. He realized now that he in no way wanted to be connected to or working for Stanton. However, he now knew that he did not want to just pack up and leave this part of the world. He was looking at Eve. Hers was such a sad story and he wondered greatly that so much depth had been hidden from his view over the last few months as he had been in her company. She had always appeared so content and perhaps not particularly elated with happiness but firmly seated in an inner joy. He now understood that this was perhaps from a deeper connection with God. Yet, she was grieving, he could see that. He wondered greatly at the woman before him. Could she really be hearing from God? Could such a burden be the cause of her sorrow?

He looked away from her, back to the beam and the little ray of light, and he realized he could probably get two fingers through the hole. He picked at the pebbles around it and found they moved easily. He looked up at the beam and around the other side. The security of the beam rested on the ground, not the wall around it. He began, gently to pull away, bit by bit, rock and dirt, until he could fit his hand through the hole.

The chain on Eve's wrist was heavy. As she fought to be free she realized she was actually wrestling with God. Looking down at the solid black links Eve saw her dreams, remembering, in progression, images, some terrible while others were promises of someone to come. For so long she had fought against her hope, because of Josiah. Eve had been promised another love, but only now as this chain linked her to

Mr. Bates did she begin to see that her dreams had already linked her to him in quite another way, by great Design. There was a part of her that would only come to know this once her love for him had fully blossomed in the present time. Until then she could not see that she already loved this man for her love had been birthed in an unconventional way. So she continued to wrestle against the chain, her mind not being able to accept being so intimately connected to someone. It was hard for her to understand that love, like every good thing, comes from God and what she felt for Mr. Bates was a feeling not conjured up by mortal inclination, nor was it the result of circumstances. It had been set in her by her Maker. Eve sighed, not a tormented weary sigh, but a tired contented sigh. She had stopped crying not because she was done, but her heart had moved past tears into a different atmosphere of sorrow. Still, as she ran her fingers along the chain, she knew no amount of tears would break it. She had learned, the will of God was like that, becoming an iron scepter to those who could not see the love behind it. So, it was that as she prayed for release for her present captivity, that God answered her, and sent a sweet spirit of peace and acceptance, that would better help her accept His will for her, easing the torment of her chains of doubt and disbelief rather than those of iron which would be broken soon enough.

God managed to calm her as few others could and feeling a bit better she turned and noticed what Mr. Bates was doing, her mind eager for anything that could possibly change their situation. Bates had continued to work but it was rough, some stones were large and unmoving but eventually a jagged and uneven opening grew. He soon found he could only dig so far back with his hands. Eve as well had begun to dig from her side and soon thought she could fit through. Sliding on her belly she wiggled, crawling on her elbows, dirt raining down on her. Mr. Bates offered her his hand but she was able to stand on her own once her feet passed through.

They were now able to move about free of the wall, Mr. Bates took the lamp and they began to head farther down the shaft.

They traveled down the shaft for hours, not knowing that Tommy hadn't taken as long to miss Mr. Bates as they had thought. While in town he happened to run into Eve's mother who informed him of Lee's troubles and that Eve had been sent with a message; so, rather than going straight over the ridge, Tommy had gone back to the mine to see if Mr. Bates was going today or not. Once he found the blocked shaft he wasted no time. He ran down to the river and gathered some men and sent word to Mr. Stanton and then led the party back to the shaft.

It was dark in the mine. Mr. Bates had turned down the flame of the lantern to try to conserve the oil. Eve, didn't mean to, but she stumbled as she felt herself tiring. Mr. Bates stopped and lifting the lantern asked if she was alright. Eve nodded, "I'm just tired and thirsty, bound in chains and lost in the dark. I'm fine. How are you?" He smiled and said, "We could stop and rest." Eve shook her head, "I want to get out of here." she said and turned her face from the glow of the flame. She was worn out. She glanced at Mr. Bates who was looking up into the darkness. The steady sound of his breathing was comforting, and when he spoke to her his voice softened in a way that caused her heart to flutter. She wondered at how familiar he seemed to her at times, as if, perhaps…but she was taken out of such thoughts as he lowered the lantern and held it behind him. "Do you see that Eve?" he asked. She looked and when he pointed up into the corner, she took a step closer to him so she could follow his line of sight. Then she saw it, a faint, but real glimmer of light, coming from above.

Mr. Bates reached for the light and grabbed an edge and pulled, now they could see a fist sized patch of blue sky. Mr. Bates worked on pushing rather than digging. Clumps of earth were moved out and soon Eve was able to climb out. Her arm was still bound but she knelt on a patch of grass and looked around. Mr. Bates was asking her what she saw, but she didn't answer immediately. The trees had been thinned, as if the place had been logged in the last twenty years. Her face flooded with recognition and she turned back to the hole, "I think I know where we are!" A few more minutes of pulling and digging saw Mr. Bates free from the mine as well. They stood and looking around Eve pointed down the hill. "We've come through the mountain. A mile or two that way and we should find Blue Cloud's village." Mr. Bates looked around and asked, "Well, do you think they'll have something to eat?" Eve noticed how very dirty Mr. Bates was and took a hand and wiped earth from her face. "Well, we're not really dressed for dinner." Mr. Bates looked at her and they laughed a good sweet laugh of achieved freedom. Their journey through the dark had not hurt them, it had only given them an opportunity to get to know each other a bit better and neither of them were sure what to do with the feelings the encounter had encouraged.

They're arrival at the Native camp caused a bit of a commotion. It wasn't everyday they saw a white man and woman, chained together, and covered in dirt. It was nearly dinner time and the sun was beginning to descend into the hills. The chief approached and looked them over. Mr. Bates was talking to Little Beaver's father, Talking Bear. "We were trapped in the mine. The shaft led us out this side of the mountain." Talking Bear picked up the chain that hung from their hands and looked at Eve. She answered as best as she could, "We were knocked out by some men we think were prospecting illegally in the mine." Eve noticed Pale Moon and nodded and turning to Mr. Bates said, "Mr. Bates, this is Pale Moon, chief of the River People." To Pale Moon she said, "This is John Bates, a builder of dams and bridges." Pale Moon looked intently at the stranger and then to the horizon and said, "The day is late and you are tired. You will stay with us tonight. I will send a messenger to the town for you to let your family know you are safe," followed by the name they had given Eve in their own language. Then he turned and walked away without another word. Talking Bear was still examining the chain, "I think I know who can help with this." he said.

The best hope was a metal spike and hammer. In the end the chain was broken. The old man who had the tools spoke to some extent in his native tongue to Talking Bear, as he fitted the spike and hammered away. Eve might have wondered more about what was said, if she hadn't been so very tired, and if for some reason the breaking of the chain hadn't caused her to feel something she didn't want to acknowledge. It was a type of sorrow, a small distant cousin to the grief she had come to know so well. And she tried to dismiss it as soon as she recognized it for what it was. Sorrow indeed had come to her again, as she thought of being unshackled from Mr. Bates.

The chain fell from his wrist first, and then Eve's arm was placed on the stump. Mr. Bates stood rubbing his lower arm and watching with curiosity the way the old man spoke, then dropped the hammer, spoke on, then dropped the hammer again. Talking Bear was smiling softly to the man's comments. What he was saying went something like this... "When I was young the river flowed and we spent our days catching the fish," *pound* "these men come and search for shiny metals that are no good to eat," *pound* "I do not understand these men." *pound, pound* "When I was a young man, if I had been chained to a pretty girl in the mountain" *pound* "I would have made her mine and brought her out as my wife." *pound* "But look at him, he will act as if their time tied together had no effect on him" *pound* "The woman will do the same. They are very strange." And with that last comment Eve's chain was released and giving them each a quizzical look he dropped the black links and shaking his hands of the matter, walked back into his dwelling.

Talking Bear led them to his wife who was cooking a meal. The smell of food brought Eve and Mr. Bates out of a tired fog. While they ate the sun passed from their view and they sat around a main fire and listened to the elders tell stories. Chief Pale Moon was particularly interested in Mr. Bates and his work with the dam and thought it a good thing to tell Mr. Bates of the history of the river and valley. They heard stories of the salmon that used to come and spawn here, and the bears they had hunted-who also fed on the salmon. Mr. Bates couldn't help but be caught in the spell of these people who seemed to be so capable of living upon and occupying the earth without disturbing the natural order of things. Across the firelight, he caught a glimpse of Eve. He noticed her wiping her face and watched as she stood, turned, and walked beyond where he could see. She seemed troubled and he went to see that she was alright.

Eve hadn't gone far, only barely beyond the edge of the firelight. She was holding a thick blanket around her shoulders as she looked up into the night sky. "Are you alright?" Eve turned at the sound of Mr. Bates' voice. She looked down and shook her head, "Um, no, it's just been a bit of a day, hasn't it?" Mr. Bates answered, "Yes, it has." Eve struggled to control her emotions. She glanced back toward the fire and the people, seeing them took away the feeling of being alone with Mr. Bates. "I'm sorry, I just wasn't prepared for the effect being here would have on me." Mr. Bates prompted her, "What do you mean?" Eve took in a deep breath and went on, "Well, I've dreamt of them too." She said, nodding toward the people. "I've heard their cries, I've met some of their fathers, not here... in my dreams. God has better promises for them than this. But it's like everything He does. The suffering must come first then the promise." Eve wiped her face again with edge of the blanket. It was getting cold out and there was so much more she wanted to say, but felt she couldn't. Looking up she watched the night and prayed that someday he might be able to understand. A lingering, yet comfortable silence fell on the two of them and long past when he could have stepped back, he stayed beside her. There was no apparent reason for it, except that he couldn't seem to leave her out there by herself.

Mr. Bates looked at her in the dark, her face toward the moon that hung high above them. She seemed as much a part of the land here as the trees and grass that made this place distinct. She seemed to belong to this place and he found that captivating to behold.

Mr. Bates looked down, his heart felt full, like a great weight of 'knowing' had been dropped on him. God had greater purposes in them all, didn't He? He felt himself wondering what his place in the grand scheme really was. Looking up at her he saw her smiling at him, a sweet smile of encouragement, her eyes shining in the dark. She looked into his eyes, those piercing blue eyes that were catching the firelight. The intensity of his gaze was not full of romantic notion. Eve saw that his soul had been touched by sadness as well and she felt herself a fool for nursing her hurt to the point of forgetting that grief was not her burden alone. Though her circumstances were her own, loss was common to all.

Eve's lip trembled. She so badly wanted to tell him everything, her whole story and what she believed was his part in it, but she couldn't, not yet, and she accepted that like she had accepted everything else that her Father had placed upon her. Eve lifted her face to the sky hoping to keep the tears from rolling down her face.

Mr. Bates felt more than he could know how to express. The immensity of God and his dealings with this simple woman in the American frontier baffled him. He didn't want to leave her feeling alone, but he was very aware of a holy fear rising within him. He became aware of God's watching gaze and he was very desirous of not over stepping any bounds of intimacy with her. He was saved from deciding what he should do as the drums began to pound and Eve looked up and said, "We should get back." But before she turned to leave she looked intently at him, "Thank you." was all she managed to say. He nodded and she smiled and walked back toward the fire.

Talking with Mr. Bates had put the Chief in a good mood. His mind and heart had been stirred by the idea that the dam was not a permanent fixture in the land, but perhaps only a temporary structure. He called for the drums and dancing that they might bless this place that it may once again be a land that honored the Maker. Mr. Bates and Eve sat and watched the figures seemingly float around the fire. Little Beaver came and sat in Eve's lap for a time and after having a quiet conversation with her he got up and moved over to Mr. Bates. He stood and inspected the newcomer for a moment and wanting to get a closer look, climbed in his lap. Mr. Bates didn't seem to mind. He continued to watch what was passing for a few minutes, while Little Beaver watched him and then occasionally looked back to Eve with a thoughtful expression on his little face. Mr. Bates was finally accosted by two small hands on the sides his face which gently turned his face down toward Little Beaver's. Mr. Bates looked into the deep brown eyes of the child and after a moment Little Beaver asked with a childlike innocence that masked the depth of understanding the question contained. "You're going to catch my dream catcher, aren't you?"

PART 7

Woe is me for my hurt!
My wound is grievous:
But I said, truly this is a grief,
and I must bear it. (h)

The eagle sees a nation red,
by land and river once was fed.
Another sings in tones of blue,
and remembers long heartaches too true.
Land conquered by the nation white,
through the sorrow, there is Light.
All nations gathered three in one;
that we see- Father, Spirit, and the Son.

The horse's hooves cut deep into the dark mud trail that wound up the mountain side. Lee led the way with John following, Blue Cloud in the rear, then the pack mule. Low hanging clouds hung as fog through the woods and John couldn't shake the cold that numbed his fingers and toes. It had only been a couple of days since Eve and Mr. Bates had been trapped in the mine, and Mr. Bates was filled with a fresh desire to discover what had caused the old foreman to leave Stanton's employ. It took them the better part of the morning but soon small wooden cabins and shacks began to appear as they entered into the heart of a rustic mining camp. Lee rode his horse up to a shack, in front of which a man had been sitting tending a small fire. Upon seeing them the man rose and stood stoic and silent as they tied the horses.

Lee walked over and greeted the man. "Good morning Brian." Brian Cuthright answered, "Morning, Lee." Brian leaned over and spit. "Wasn't expecting to see you today." Lee shook his hand "Yeah, well, I've brought you an Englishman." He turned toward John, "Brian this is John Bates, he's an engineer. Stanton brought here to look over the mine and dam." John extended his hand and Brian cautiously took it. Mr. Cuthright was a lean, strong looking man despite the years his graying beard testified of. He eyed Mr. Bates warily, convinced no good thing ever came from the general direction of Trevor Stanton. "Well, what can we do for you Mr. Bates?" he asked with reserved hospitality. He turned and motioned for the men to sit on the logs and stumps that served as seats around the fire. John sat, but Lee excused himself and went to help Blue Cloud unload the mule. A few small children, dirty, but happy came screaming, "Grandpa, grandpa!" and after being hugged, began tearing into the bundles.

John turned back to Brian. "Well, to be honest with you, Mr. Stanton led me to believe that he feared for the dam because of an accident that happened there, but I've come to find out that was years ago." Brian let out an exhale of disgust, then grew thoughtful. He spit on the ground before speaking, "You think that there's anything wrong with that dam?" he asked as he stretched out his leg to get more comfortable. Mr. Bates decided to be very straight forward with the man, "Maybe. But there are a great number of homes and livelihoods sitting in the path of that river, and there are those who are not convinced that's a safe place to have a town. I'm inclined to agree. No matter how sound the dam seems at the moment. If I'm to try to persuade them to move to higher ground, I'm going to need all the facts I can get." This revelation surprised and intrigued Cuthright who then stood looking down on Mr. Bates. He seemed to be calculating the full worth of the new comer. He raised his head, the brim of his hat letting go of a drop of water as he did, and looking up the hillside he said, "Let's take a walk, Mr. Bates."

Mr. Cuthright seemed to have lost all of his cautionary reserve and was now talking freely as he guided Mr. Bates up a small trail. "This side of the mountain is still open country, men are free to prospect and stake their own claims." John was curious, "How long have you been out here?" Brian stepped over a log, "There's been a small community of dreamers living out here for years, I only came out and joined them a little over a year ago." Mr. Bates added, "After the cave in?" Brian stopped, his eye brows raised, wondering how much Mr. Bates had heard. "Yeah." he said and again gazed at John, as if taking an inventory of the man's metal. He went on, "I nearly lost a good man that day, but all Mr. Stanton seemed to care about was the shaft we lost." He sighed and looked John straight in the eyes. "You ever seen a man on the edge of death?" He wasn't really asking for particulars of Mr. Bates' life, simply turning the focus of the conversation. "I was never a church going man though my folks taught me how to read out of the family Bible, but that day changed my life. I saw a man's breath taken right out of him." He stopped walking at the top of a small rise and continued. "It was a normal day, just like any other, searching for shine in the belly of the earth. A support blew out, it happened suddenly, without warning." Brian seemed to be rolling things around on his tongue for a moment and stroked his beard. When he looked back his voice was choked with emotion. "After that, I just couldn't do it; diving into unsafe depths, risking lives. For what? Nothing but a bit of shine. The mine or the dam, that's not the problem down there, it's the people." He turned and continued on while he spoke. John strode up beside him so he could hear. "I'd been wearing thin for years. That was just the last straw. I saw men who earned good money choosing to spend it on the whores, or lose it playing cards, rather than building proper houses for their families. So the town built up more saloons, choosing to invest in getting their money back rather than building a proper school." They had come to an opening in the trees and over a small ridge the town could be seen in the distance. Frontier lay nestled in the valley, the fog clutching at it like white clawing fingers. Brian continued as he motioned in that direction, "It wears away on ya, bit by bit, until finally I look down and I can hardly see a trace of the good countryside my father decided to settle in." Mr. Bates looked at Cuthright, it was a sad thing to see, a man who had lost his good opinion of his home. Yet, Brian didn't seem overly bitter. He was simply raked thin with discouragement and heartache. The years had been hard on him. Life in this place, Mr. Bates was seeing, was hard for those who chose not to be led astray by the quick and easy pay off. Few took the harder path toward the fertile soil of struggle and survival that bred strong character and true faith.

Brian turned back to the trail and Mr. Bates and said nothing. They went on for some time and finally Brian breached another topic. "I heard you met Eve Carson a few days back." Mr. Bates looked up. Brian had stopped and turned his eyes burning into John with an intensity he wasn't prepared for. Mr. Bates drew up and faced the miner and Brian nodded, "I'm just going to say this once, I'm not particularly a church fella, but that woman sometimes knows things only God could have told her." His eyes dropped and he stood quietly, as if remembering. Mr. Bates spoke, "Well I must say some of her comments did give me pause to go back and take another look at the mine." Brian asked, "Why do I get the feeling that your talking with her has more to do with your interest in moving the town than what you've seen of the dam?" Mr. Bates answered, "She does have a rather interesting perspective. I went back and looked at the original plans and found some discrepancies. There are supports that appear on the plans that I cannot find in the dam, as if they just weren't made to last. It is troubling and I cannot function under the assumption that the dam is sound. It now seems to me to be holding in spite of the fact that it should have breached years ago." Brian hmmmed and nodding he lifted an arm up and leaned against a small tree, looking back toward town through the trees.

"And talking to Mrs. Carson is what made you go back and take a second look?" Looking toward the town he spoke, "The town's got to do the same. They need to take another look at what really matters." The eminent problems of the many lives below seemed a simple topic of discussion from this mountain top, "So do you really think you can convince them to pull up stakes and move to higher ground?" Mr. Bates followed his gaze, he desperately hoped so, but in his experience people could often be reluctant to sacrifice so much for something that would perhaps be the benefit of future generations. Without a present threat would the town move to save their children and grandchildren from facing the same problem? He only suspected that the dam hadn't been built according to the plans. Without tearing into it, he had no actual proof, so he stated honestly, "Some perhaps, but I'm afraid there are those who won't be moved no matter how much supporting evidence I can muster. The dam has to break for us to be proved right. How do we convince them before it's too late?"

Clear it seems, yet thin as glass,
how quickly certainty can pass
I tell you truly, but you won't see,
to higher ground you all must flee
But on old hopes you choose to stand,
in homes you built on sinking sand.

John was splashing water on his face, rinsing away the last traces of a beard. He was preparing to meet with Mr. Stanton, perhaps for the last time. His heart and conscious were weighing heavily within his being. He was an engineer yet, there were those here who were hoping to find in him some kind of savior. Slipping on a clean shirt he looked out the window as he buttoned it up. This journey had not been what he had expected. His mind's eye flooded with images of Eve, his meeting her had seemed to change everything and yet nothing, the sensation was disturbing.

A letter sat, folded neatly, although it had been opened and read, on a small table that was serving as his desk in the corner of the room. He glanced at it as he sat on the bed and pulled his shoes out and began putting them on. He knew his mind should be focused on the dam and Stanton. This conversation had to go well. If he couldn't convince Stanton to relocate the town, few would follow the word of a stranger. He remembered what Eve had said about Stanton and he grew angry. Stanton probably deserved to drown in the flood. He sighed. He didn't want to see anyone living beneath that dam, even Stanton. His thoughts turned to Lee, perhaps through the church some could be convinced. Thinking of Lee brought him back around to Eve. He reached over and picked up the letter. Unfolding it, he read it again, as he had done so many times in the past three days. Refolding the paper with disturbed reverence he placed it back on the table where it would remain in his line of sight.

Eve pulled the wagon up in front of the store. She had just deposited her children at the school house. They had arrived a bit early, but Eve had been eager to move on and perhaps miss seeing Marie Swanson who lately could only talk about the tall Englishman who had come to town. Usually Eve would have visited Miss Ruth before purchasing her groceries. Today she wasn't sure she wanted to risk running into Mr. Bates again. She found she couldn't help thinking of him, despite all she did to avoid even the mention of his name. Her dreams could not seem to be spared his presence lately either. With everything she had been through, she should have been pliable and obedient to the gentle nudging of the Holy Spirit. But she found herself struggling, yet again with the intangible nature of the revelations and the unprecedented journey of love woven within it. She was interested in this new man who had suddenly appeared in her life and that irritated her beyond reason.

Entering the store, she found that although the large room was practically empty, the atmosphere was completely filled with the presence of Miss Marie Swanson who must have stopped in on her way to the school house. Eve steeled herself and tried not to hear Miss Swanson's conversation with Mrs. Brown who was tending the counter. The two of them nodded at Eve but went on as if she wasn't there. The store wasn't that large so Eve was soon affronted by their exchange. Mrs. Brown was saying, in a hushed tone at first, "But I thought you and Mr. Stanton would have some kind of understanding by now?" Miss Swanson replied, "Well, so did I, but if he's not going to ask, well I'm not above setting my cap elsewhere. Lord knows I've got too much sense to pin all my hopes on a man who hasn't asked me after all this time." Mrs. Brown tried to warn her, "But there's no telling how long that Mr. Bates will be in town for. What if he decides there's nothing to be done with the dam after all?" Eve could see Miss Swanson skake her head a bit at this, "Well, he's a catch that'd be worth the risk. And if nothing comes of it, perhaps a little competition is just what Mr. Stanton needs to warm up those cold feet of his." Mrs. Brown didn't seem to approve, "It's a dangerous game you're playing my dear, be careful. Many a girl has lost the affections of a good man by playing trifle with his feelings."

The bell on the door rang again as someone entered. From where she stood Eve saw Mr. Bates first and found herself ducking into the aisle out of sight. She rolled her eyes at her own behavior, why did she care? Miss Swanson turned and upon seeing who it was she called out, "Hello, there Mr. Bates, what a delight to see you here this morning." Mr. Bates tipped his hat and made a polite, yet distracted reply to her and Mrs. Brown and then glanced around the rest of the store. He had stepped into the store on a sudden whim, for he had recognized Lee's team parked out front.

Miss Swanson had no care for why Mr. Bates had entered. She was set on making the most of a meeting with him. "So how are you getting along with your work, Mr. Bates?" She asked innocently as she drew near to him. Mr. Bates reconciled himself to a conversation, "Slowly, I must say. I'm to have a meeting with Mr. Stanton today actually to discuss what direction the town should take." Miss Swanson was determined to flash a winning smile no matter how droll she found the topic. "Why, Mr. Bates you do seem so very serious what can we do to lighten your mood?" Mr. Bate smiled slightly, flushed by her flirtation, "I wish very much I had time for more social visits, but I find Mr. Stanton is right to be concerned about the dam." He moved to say good day to the ladies and make his escape, but Miss Swanson was formidable. She gently grabbed his arm and pulling him back went on, "Oh, dear. Do you really think there is any danger, Mr. Bates?" She had pulled them closer to the stove, which was putting out a good deal of heat and her cheeks began to flush.

Mr. Bates began to answer her question when raising a hand to her head Miss Swanson swooned. Mr. Bates was quick to catch her lowering her gently to the floor. Mrs. Brown came running around the counter with a cool glass of water. The two of them hovered over Miss Swanson. "Oh dear me, Mr. Bates, I'm afraid she overheated being so close to the fire. She just needs a bit of cool water." Mr. Bates cradled her head in his hands, and Miss Swanson's eyes fluttered as she lay in his arms.

Water crashed down, a whole cupful, and instantly Miss Swanson was animated, her face cooled of flush from the fire, but horribly distorted in anger and surprise. Mr. Bates looked up to see Eve standing over them, Mrs. Brown's empty glass in her hand. Eve glanced at the three of them as they looked at her in silent shock, "Well, Mrs. Brown was right a touch of cold water did the trick." Then placing the glass on the nearest shelf she vanished out the door.

Mr. Bates draped a hand across his face to hide his smile. He could hardly keep from laughing. He and Mrs. Brown helped an irate Miss Swanson to her feet. "Well I never! That Eve Carson! I tell you Mr. Bates, she's gone half mad." Mrs. Brown was amazed at Miss Swanson's remark, "Marie!" she scolded, "Eve Carson is a gentle soul," then looking to Mr. Bates while Miss Swanson wiped her face, she added, "No doubt she had her reasons for behaving as she did." And let her eyes roll over Miss Swanson with an apparent disapproval of the woman's man catching techniques.

Eve sat in amazement as Miss Ruth burst out laughing. "Bless you child!" she called out before her laughter overwhelmed her. "I wish I could have seen it." She managed to say in between joyful ripples. Eve sat in disbelief; she had thought her behavior would merit some kind of reprimand. She didn't find any part of what she had done to be amusing. But Miss Ruth soon helped her along, "I can just see lil' Miss Prim and Proper. She musta looked like a cat after it's slipped into a trough, all angry for losing all its fluff and being seen for what it is." She clapped her hands and rolled on again, this time Eve had to bow her head as her own amusement took root and bubbled up inside of her. She still couldn't believe what could have possessed her to do that. She and Miss Swanson had never been close. It was hard for Eve to take her seriously on any matter. But she was the children's teacher and they had, up until now, had a pleasant acquaintance.

Eve slumped in her chair and laid her head in her hand. Miss Ruth was gaining control of herself as Eve stated, "I don't know what I was thinking, I'm going to have to apologize. Oh!

It's so humiliating." Miss Ruth went stone silent at this and Eve glanced up and saw her friend gazing at her with an open and knowing look. Leaning forward Ruth took her friend's face in her hands and made Eve look straight as her, "Child, sometimes the absurdity of this whole life just causes us to need to burst out and let loose once in a while. You ain't done nothing that's worth all them tears."

Eve looked up at her in desperation, "I feel wrong, it feels wrong to… to see him, to know that maybe he is… to feel…" Eve looked away her face getting hot again. Miss Ruth dropped her chin and thought about the right words. Leaning forward she took Eve by the hands, "I know it feels wrong, honey, but when God does something special it always goes against the natural way, because it's done His way. I've heard you pray Eve. I been here on my knees right beside you in times of grief and you know what I heard? I heard a woman with a heart for God, crying out for help when you couldn't handle all He was showing you. I heard you asking Him to take this pain, this burden He put on you…but then you went on praying because a part of you understands that this is from Him and that part of you dared to say, if this is from you God then don't take it, just give me the strength to bear it, to get through it." Miss Ruth took a deep breath and waited. Eve lifted her head and looked up at her friend. Eve's tears spilled over and Miss Ruth wiped them away and said, "He gave you what you asked for just not in the way you expected. He gave you a glimpse of what was coming, and now he came…that's all there is to it. You don't have to do anything, just trust, just trust."

There was no escape. In order to keep any shred of balance she needed to let go of what she 'thought' was wrong with her thoughts about Mr. Bates. She couldn't help the way she was feeling, it was overwhelming. She was learning her own strength and the fact that she was functioning through it all taught her something about herself she hadn't known before. Eve relied greatly on her morality, on her understanding of what was good and right. Being a sensitive and feeling person she had learned to trust her knowledge of God to teach her what was right and wrong, rather than the emotions that rose and fell within her sweet or sad. The present situation, however, was asking her to trust completely in a God she couldn't fully comprehend. Trust him down a path that seemed both painful and lovely beyond anything she had dared to believe possible before. God had awakened love before she could embrace it so she could gain a promise and strength to keep moving, keep living. This woman was lost in the wilderness that is 'the audacity of the Almighty', and she was beginning to truly know Him as never before. She stood and left the room. Entering the wash room she cooled the flush of her cheeks and as she stood up from drying her face, saw her reflection in the mirror.

Eve had never considered herself beautiful. She still felt very much the shy and awkward child that she had once been. In her youth she had at times thought she had achieved some level of "pretty". Her features were fair, her eyes and hair brown but in truth whenever she looked into a mirror she saw only herself.

Tenderly she lifted her fingers and traced her eyebrow. It was well shaped, but then she moved to her lower lid. Years of life, laughter and tears had left their mark there. Her fingers continued their travels down her cheek and to her lips, they were full but in this moment Eve could only perceive that. She had lost her composure and the events of the morning were causing her to reflect on her own reflection in an unsavory light. She perceived nothing in that pane of glass that could catch the eye or heart of anyone after Josiah. The mirror spoke nothing to her about the way her laugh carried in a room, or the beauty of her smile, nor could it show her the way she lit up when the one she loved was in the room. All these things now seemed out of place as she thought of Josiah. They had met when they were just into their twenties, so young and starry eyed about love and wishing to start a family together. She wrung the towel out and hung it up. Why!? Again, she shouted to her inner self, why do I care!? She had thrown that cold water on Miss Swanson for one reason alone, she had felt protective of Mr. Bates. A bit jealous, but she wouldn't let herself consider the cause of such a feeling, instead she churned it over into self- chiding for allowing herself to be moved by such a petty feeling. She had simply wanted to be spared the pain of seeing him in the company of another woman, selfish and painful as the realization was, it was the truth. Pausing she glanced back at the mirror and gazed into her eyes. They began to call to memory her dreams, the image she had seem so many times the image of a man, who caused her heart to beat again. In this waking world she could only summon a whisper of the feeling like a gentle breeze that could only cause a leaf to turn over but lacked the power to lift it off the ground. Her heart could not summon the feeling, or her memory the face of her dream of love. There were similarities, Eve had to admit, more than admit, she could not deny. It was as if markers along a roadside had been laid down so that she could find her way, but they had been hidden within the shrubs of her dreams. Mr. Bates had turned them over one by one, catching her attention, drawing parallels, connecting her dreams to the real world without even knowing it and disrupting her illusions that all these things would come at a much later time. Eve had recognized him from the very first moment of their meeting and the strangeness of the encounter was bothersome. Often his presence alone would trigger images she had seen in her dreams. She found herself irritated that she could not better control her heart and thoughts on the matter. Her rational mind was jumping to conclusions because her heart had been awakened despite her best attempts at resisting. And she was in a state of shock, for Mr. Bates' coming had been well before she had seriously thought it was appropriate to actually be watching for the man from her dreams.

Looking at herself she began to think, *"I'm so broken. I'm shattered." Leaning on the basin she took a closer look, "Not a normal brokenness caused only by tragedy, but I'm deeply broken a break that was caused by foreknowledge. All from a God who I know to be unfathomably good. Even if my heart could love again, what kind of person am I now? What will the cost for this lesson be? Can I trust God in this, the strangeness of all this?* Eve felt tired. She didn't want to 'know' anymore, she truly just wished that God would let her heart rest and leave her in peace for a time.

When she re-entered the kitchen and sat down, Miss Ruth put a cup of tea down in front of her and sat across from her friend lifting her chin so that their eyes met. Her friend and counselor sat before her, a true looking glass, revealing the unmasked truth that the bathroom glass had not the capacity to know.

Miss Ruth sat back and the motion was not only physical, it was as if she was able to pull the entire atmosphere of the room *deeper* into contemplation. Eve found herself feeling as if she was more in this moment, in the now. Miss Ruth pursed her lips as if she was rolling a taste around in her mouth, savoring the flavor, trying to discover what each individual ingredient was, as only a master in the kitchen could. Finally, she decided she had contemplated enough to speak.

"Eve, you need to understand that a passage of time is not necessary in order for us to love someone. And in the same moment you need to reconcile yourself to the fact that God lives 'outside' of time as we know it."

Eve was holding a hankie to her cheek and looked up in wonder at her friend. She knew this was true, but her fear had been shrouding it from view.

Miss Ruth went on, "Love isn't meant to be a fall, child. A fall is what cost mankind the Garden of Paradise. Love is meant to be a leap, in obedience, in the direction God has shown you to leap. Most people come to realize they love someone over time, that's a normal everyday kind of love. But you've got something special. God has been pouring love into you, awaking your love ahead of time, because you need it to get through your sorrow. All that's happened now is He's shown you that you're gonna leap in *this* direction. Now, you need to take hold of that. But rest in the now, cause it ain't time to jump yet, just to 'know'. I can't imagine what you're going through, girl, but I do know God wouldn't ask something of you that you couldn't do, you can hold this Eve, you can hold this for now."

Eve bowed her head. Softly she dared to utter, "I'm afraid, Ruth. I'm afraid of myself. I'm not ready for these feelings."

Miss Ruth nodded, "I know what you're afraid of, child, and bless you for it. You doubt yourself, but God doesn't. He wouldn't be showing this, revealing this to you now unless He had given you all you need to carry it. Trust. All you need is trust. You want to understand. You want it to all make sense. But God is working on your faith and that is something the rational mind cannot make sense of. Remember Mary, she 'carried these things in her heart', and you're being asked to do the same."

Eve looked at her trembling hands. She could see the palace of her heart surrounded by all those lovely bubbles of her dreams. It stood a glistening tower of soft rounds, each a different expression of promise. Did she have enough confidence that this man was the one she had been told of to let that palace of dreams burst so that something in this reality could take its place?

Miss Ruth spoke up, "Everything is gonna change, girl. Everything but one, God still loves you, and He'll still be with you, no matter what."

Eve sat very still, a thousand feelings and thoughts, maybes and might nots were running through her. She couldn't know how Mr. Bates felt or what might happen, God alone had to be her foundation. Did she trust Him, even when He exposed her heart to that perilous emotion of love?

Trevor Stanton asked with a mocking smile, "What do you mean, 'you can't fix it?'" He went on with decided authority, "I hired you to come here and fix the dam." Mr. Bates was sorry that Mr. Stanton was going to be so disappointed. "I am sorry to have to tell you this, Mr. Stanton, but it is my opinion that the dam is simply no longer capable of holding the increasing water levels. The land is changing and the dam can't hold it back anymore. It's going to fail. It's only a matter of time." Mr. Stanton rocked back in his chair, as if chewing on this, "So you're saying nothing can be done, the dam, my mine, this town...it's all just done for?" Stanton couldn't believe the apparent abandonment this man was exhibiting toward his home. Mr. Bates was trying to express his great concern for the matter. "The town, as far as the buildings and houses go yes, but your community can and I believe will survive. You will simply need to make a fresh start of it." Mr. Stanton grew very serious, "A fresh start? Do you know how much my family has poured into the making of this town? This place represents our sweat, our blood. We braved the elements, we conquered the mountain, we fought off the Indians…" Mr. Bates couldn't listen anymore, "But you won't be able to hold back that river. Water, in that volume, is capable of changing the face of the earth in a sudden and violent way, Mr. Stanton. You have to start relocating to the hills."

Mr. Stanton stood up out of his chair and paced around his desk. He looked out the window to those very hills, "You know those hills are where the first missionaries lived." He turned, "They lived in tents, dependent on help from those savages. You're asking me to give up." Sitting on the front corner of the desk he crossed his arms and leaned into Mr. Bates face, "Well, I'm not going to do that." He stated slowly and pointedly.

Mr. Bates blinked, and started shaking his head, "Mr. Stanton, I don't think you quite understand…"

Stanton cut him off, "Oh, I understand alright." His voice trembling with contained rage, "You've had your holiday with the Indians, and the church's little lambs, you've even made buddy- buddy with that old coot of a miner, and they've all convinced you that the big bad Trevor Stanton's got-ta go. But I'll go out and find a better engineer who'll be more than happy to fix my problem."

Now Mr. Bates rose to his feet, "Mr. Stanton, there is a very real and pressing danger. It was a very heavy winter and with spring upon you that river is going to continue to rise, I know it's not what you want to hear, but you are in a very real danger if you remain in this valley. This dam worked, for a time, but times change."

Mr. Stanton dipped his head in contemplation, and when he looked up, his eyes flickered almost as flames. "Now, you listen to me. I've got eyes all over this town and I know where your head's at. You think you can build a better town, one that's not full of the greed and corruption my family brought in. But let me tell you, I won't have it. This country, it's in its infancy and it takes money and power to advance civilization. If that mine goes so will the town. The silver from that mine is what built this town and without it there will be nothing here but a handful of squatters who'll have to play nice with Native's just to survive."

Mr. Bates was at a loss for words. Mr. Stanton was willing to risk his own life and the lives of others in order to hold onto a small town on the outskirts of the civilized world. Anything that was of true value or worth here was in the people, not in the things they had built. He let out long slow sigh of defeat, "I'm very sorry you feel that way, Mr. Stanton. But you have to understand that my conscience does not allow me to be silent. I'm going to tell the people of the town to move to higher ground as soon as possible."

Mr. Stanton stood up slowly and placed his hands in his pockets. "Now I'm very sorry that you feel that way, Mr. Bates. And I should warn you that if you go around, and try to spread a panic through our peaceful existence," he paused and flashed his most charming smile, "I'm going to have you run out of my town. And if it comes to that, I promise you," as he pointed his finger in the shape of a gun and bounced it gently off Mr.

Bates chest, "the dam failing is going to be the least of your worries."

PART 8

*"...God, who...calls those things
which do not exist as though they did..."* [i]

Calls ring out, the time has come
to stir the hearts, Your will be done
Builder, Prophet, Father, Son
Mother, Daughter, Love in one.

Eve had made a rather awkward apology to Miss Swanson when she picked the kids up from school. Now, Sammy was sitting on the buck board rattling on about school that day, while his mother listened, rather inattentively. "And then Bobby caught the biggest mouse, ever, out in the wood shed, and showed us the best way to kill a mouse. You just fling it against the door jam and knock it out, then you just stomp on its head. Just one good stomp kills it just like that." Eve gave a half smile to her son's exuberance for becoming a mighty mouse hunter. Sammy suddenly changed topics, "Hey mom, isn't that Grandpa's friend, Mr. Bates?" Sammy was pointing to the right and Eve followed his gaze and saw Mr. Bates striding down the walkway in what she had to guess was a very agitated or angry manner. Before Eve realized what Sammy was up to, he was waving and screaming. "Hey, Mr. Bates, Mr. Bates! Over here!" Mr. Bates looked up and Eve expected his expression to lighten at the sight of them, but it didn't. His face seemed set in determination as he crossed the street to their wagon while Eve pulled the team up.

"Is something wrong Mr. Bates?" she asked. He grabbed a hold of the wagon and looked up, "I'm afraid so, Mrs.

Carson. Are you headed to your father's house?" Eve shook her head slightly, his intensity throwing her off a bit, "Well, yes." Mr. Bates practically interrupted her, "Would you mind if I rode up there with you?" Eve nodded a yes, though she didn't know his purpose. She knew there must be something going on. She turned and asked Sammy to hop in the back of the wagon with his brother and sister. While he did so he was asking, "Are ya going to come for dinner Mr. Bates? I'd love to show you my sling shot..." Eve turned and smiled, "Sammy, sit down, there'll be plenty of time for that later." Mr. Bates suddenly realized he was climbing into the wagon beside her and felt his tension ease, slightly. He turned and answered Sammy's question, "If your Grandmother and Grandfather will be good enough to have me, I think I will stay for dinner." Sammy made a funny face, as if it was silly to think they'd turn him away, since he was already in the wagon, but he sat and said no more contented with the fact that he would have an opportunity to show Mr. Bates his treasures later.

They rode on in silence for a few minutes. Mr. Bates seemed lost in his thoughts, a stern look weighing his brows down as he watched the countryside slowly roll by. Eve felt silly, but spoke up anyway, "I'd like to tell you how very sorry I am, Mr. Bates, for my behavior in the store this morning." Mr. Bates turned toward her with a puzzled expression that told Eve his thoughts must have been miles away and made her wish she had said nothing about it. He soon remembered and allowed himself to laugh softly, "That's alright Mrs. Carson." He turned away and would have let the matter drop, but Julie popped up. "Momma, you'll never guess what happened to poor Miss Swanson. She showed up to school, her hair and collar soaked with water. She said an old mule was drinking in a trough as she walked by and splashed it all over her." Eve closed her eyes in painful embarrassment. Mr. Bates looked up from the child and smiled at Eve. Looking toward him Eve saw him raise an eyebrow at her; he held her children's good opinion of her in his hands. He had to comment, "Is that what she said happened?" Eve gave him a stern look not to tell them and then realized he was teasing her. She looked away and humbly answered, "I suppose I deserve that." Mr. Bates encouraged Julie to sit back and turned back in his seat and replied, "I suppose Miss Swanson deserved it, too." Eve glanced at him and couldn't help herself as the two of them shared quiet laughter.

Mr. Bates sighed. "I'm sorry I jumped into your wagon so abruptly back there, but I had a meeting with Mr. Stanton today and I'd like to talk with Lee as soon as possible." The serious tone of his voice caused Eve to give him a questioning look as she asked, "It didn't go well?" although she already knew the answer. Mr. Bates looked down at his feet, "No." he said lifting his eyes to the road ahead, "It didn't go well at all." He glanced back at the children; he didn't want to say too much in front of tiny ears. Eve glanced back as well and nodded, "I'm sure it'll keep, Mr. Bates, besides I know Trevor Stanton well enough to guess most of it."

Mr. Bates turned his gaze and again they rode on in silence as the kids talked and played in the back ground. His presence somehow found and soothed all the anxiety in her heart rather than antagonizing it.

The storm clouds had grown dark, rather suddenly, and Eve and Mr. Bates hurried the kids into the house as the rain began to pour down. Eve's mother met them inside the door and it wasn't until she had James seated on the bench and one of his boots off that she noticed Mr. Bates mixed up among her family. "Well, Mr. Bates, what are you doing up here tonight?" Mr. Bates smiled a bit sheepishly, "I'm so sorry to intrude Mrs. Wood, but I have some news I'd like to discuss with your husband, and I..." Mrs. Wood cut him off, "Well never mind, you're here now and," looking out the window she continued, "it looks like you and Blue Cloud are going to have to bunk up here for the night." Despite the fact that it was over an hour until sunset, the clouds were thick and what waning evening light they could have expected was now lost. Eve hurried the kids on out of the hall and said, "Mr. Bates, you can sit in by the fire. Would you like a cup of tea?" He said that he would and stepped into the front room.

Eve was in the kitchen with her mother pouring a cup of tea for Mr. Bates. Her mother had Julie helping her peel potatoes and asked, "Did Mr. Bates mention what's going on to you Eve?" Eve glanced at her over Julie's head and gave a slight nod, but then lowered her eyes to her daughter, then back to her mother. Eve shared all she knew, "He only said that he met with Trevor Stanton today and wanted to speak with Dad about it." Her mother knew this had the potential to be something serious, but turned her attention back to her granddaughter and pulled out a few more potatoes as Eve took Mr. Bates his tea.

Mr. Bates had taken off his wet jacket and hung it over a chair near the fire. He stood with his arms resting on the mantle, gazing into the flames. Pulling one of his hands down he looked at the letter. He had stopped at the post office that morning and found a second letter repeating the same message. Mr. Bates ran his hand through his hair. He was thinking hard about many things and didn't notice when Eve stood near the door of the room. She never felt equal to the task of seeing him, her entire being trembled with uncertainty, doubt and fear she could not contain. The cup rattled in her hand as she tried to shake all these things off and live in the 'now'. Her current situation was set, God alone was in control. She had to know much, but do nothing. Such was her path for the moment. Finding her voice she said, "Your tea, Mr. Bates." He turned, and Eve couldn't help but feel for him, his expression seemed so troubled. Taking the tea from Eve he sat in the arm chair and took a sip.

Eve wanted to speak with him, but wasn't sure what to say. The opportunity was interrupted by Sammy who came charging in the room right up to Mr. Bates. Eve had to laugh at her son; he was decked out with every toy weapon he owned. A wooden sword was tucked in his belt, his little bow and arrows were slung over his shoulder, and in his hand he held up the sling shot for inspection. "See Mr. Bates, it's a really good one too. I can hit down all the tin cans out back, I been practicing," he glanced outside at the rain and his shoulders dropped in defeat, "but I guess we can't go shooting today." Eve slid into the chair. She wanted to be able to rein him in if he began to overwhelm Mr. Bates. But Mr. Bates surprised her by showing a keen interest in the young man's arsenal. Sammy pulled off his bow and quiver and Mr. Bates inspected them showing all the appropriate admiration that they deserved. The bow was even topped off with a couple of large feathers and Mr. Bates asked, "Did Blue Cloud make this for you?" Sammy held the bow in his hands, "Nope, my dad made them. It shoots way better than the one Bobby's dad made for him." Mr. Bates smiled at the pride the boy so easily displayed for his father and glanced up to his mother. She smiled sweetly at the pair of them. Sammy had set the bow down and drew out his wooden sword, "But Grandpa made me this!" he sang and Mr. Bates had to duck as Sammy brandished it. Eve was quick to scold him, "Sammy Carson, you know better, slow down." Sammy gave his mother a submissive look and apologized to Mr. Bates who was laughing. "It's alright Sammy," as he stood and grabbing the poker from the fire, he leveled it as a sword and continued, "But you should know that where I come from, a man doesn't draw his sword unless he intends to use it." Sammy eyes danced and he attacked Mr. Bates with great enthusiasm, though little skill and Mr. Bates disarmed him quickly. Sammy stood in awe of Mr. Bates. Mr. Bates smiled and pointed the poker at the fallen wooden sword, "Pick it up and try again." Sammy picked up his sword and Eve, now confident that Mr. Bates could hold his own with her outgoing boy, retreated back into the kitchen to help with dinner.

Lee entered the front room and said, "If you've don't mind, John, I'd like to visit with you for a few minutes before dinner time." Sammy was disappointed but with a touch from his grandfather he resigned to go to the kitchen.

Lee offered Mr. Bates a chair, and then patted his pockets and turned and found his pipe on the small desk in the corner. Mr. Bates was tired and comforted by the warmth of the fire but he rubbed his hands together, wondering what Lee wanted to speak to him about.

Lee wasn't in a hurry. He sat and filled his pipe and once it was lit he flicked his match into the fire and took a good look at Mr. Bates.

"John," he began, "I want to talk to you about Eve." Mr. Bates felt nervous energy flood through him. No man looked forward to an awkward conversation with a capable frontiersman about his daughter. Lee took particular notice of Mr. Bates subtle discomposure at the mention of his daughter.

He turned his pipe in his hand and looked at it for a minute before going on. John sat silent, waiting for what Lee had to say.

Lee seemed to be searching for the right words, "Eve is well... different ." Mr. Bates blinked and thought about this. Lee continued, "I mean, few people, hear from God as she does. I wanted you to know that I suspect God's told her a thing or two about you. She's been watching and waiting and praying for this town and the dam, and I think you should perhaps be a bit more interested in what she might know about it." Mr. Bates smiled, "Well, she mentioned a few things..." Lee looked at him with great interest and Mr. Bates nodded and went on, "...when we were in the mine." Lee puffed his pipe then took it from his mouth and looked at it before letting his gaze settle on the larger fire. "Well," he finally said, "I guess I've just been curious about it, but now I think I should have remembered that she tends to be quiet about what she sees, until things happen, actually unfold, then she can put all the pieces together. I've just noticed her watching you and I've wondered at it." Mr. Bates felt a bit embarrassed. "Let me assure you..." Lee's expression was so full of amused disbelief that John stopped talking. Lee exclaimed almost under his breath, "Hell John, I have no worries on that matter and even if I did doubt your character, I know my daughter. I'm talking about destinies, and God's design in all this. He knits people together. Some people are simply set by God to be pivotal in the lives of others. That's all, it's nothing to get uncomfortable about." Lee sat back and relit his pipe, as it had gone out. Mr. Bates let out a small chuckle of relief and so very much wanted to end this conversation which he felt should not be making him as uncomfortable as it was. Lee rocked back in his chair and sighed, "No John, I'm just mulling over some things, like perhaps there is more to your being here than just that dam, and perhaps God's given Eve a message for you, some insight or knowledge. Yeah, I just think God's doing something here a bit deeper than any of us realize, that's all. And I thought you should know that Eve can talk about God and if you get a chance you should listen to what she has to say. I don't believe that God brought you here to tell us the dam was going to break, over half the town believes it could whether they'll admit it or not. I also don't believe that Eve just saw that someone was going to come here at such a time. I believe she saw you, and seeing you now in reality has shaken her. I just don't understand exactly what God's up to with all of this." Mr. Bates lowered his face and thought about it. The fire burned for another few minutes as the two men sat in contemplation.

Dreams I thought were vapor gasps,
appear too real, too hard, too fast
So many dreams, none too few...
Do you believe I saw things true?

The door opened silently and boots shuffled onto the hard floor. The sweeping breath of wind and snow accosted the fire. Lee and Mr. Bates looked up and realizing they were no longer alone. Blue Cloud stood with Josiah by his side. Lee stood up, "Well, you too were working late." Josiah took off his hat and shook the rain from it before placing it on the stand by the fire. Lee motioned toward Mr. Bates, "Josiah, have you met John." Josiah turned, "No, I haven't actually, though Eve's told me about you." As the two shook hands and exchanged pleasantries, Lee looked up and noticed Eve had entered the room. Her gaze was fixed on the hands of the two men and she was watching the meeting with interest. As her eyes lifted to her father's for a shimmering moment he thought she looked as if she might burst into tears. She steeled herself and looked away and greeted her husband and Blue Cloud. Seeing the men were all eager to chat she excused herself to fetch them some coffee. But the truth was that she felt as if she was going to be sick. She was seeing something God had whispered to her. Amid the visions of breaking water and destruction he had softly assured her there would be comfort and it would be easy and familiar. But this was more than she felt she could take. Later...if this was true he would come later, after the unthinkable happened. Seeing the two men side by side who caused her to feel things that she could only reconcile by separating them with time spun her. Leaning upon the wall she prayed for strength. What lay before her seemed beyond the goodness of God and yet, here it was and it was from Him so all her knowledge of His goodness was now being rearranged and it was a turbulent process. Beyond her own belief she found that she was able to go on with the menial task of coffee.

Josiah and Blue Cloud began to take off coats and find a seat as they started to fill Lee in on the progress of the barn's construction. They had been out trying to finish a section to hold the rain away from a stack of fresh hay.

Lee was still wondering about Eve in light of his recent observation, but couldn't help be pulled into the conversation. He did notice however, that Mr. Bates wouldn't allow himself to look back in the direction she had gone.

Trevor Stanton stood in the rain at the end of the valley. The huge dam stood a stone giant which held the fate of the town in its dimwitted hands. Water from the clouds battered upon its surface, but they broke like tears upon a gravestone. Trevor's eyes reflected the flames from his cigar and he smiled. His false hope growing the longer the dam stood in the raging storm. The dam would hold it had to. What would this valley be without that dam? Stanton didn't allow himself to think of the generations of time and peoples who had lived in this place before that dam. All he thought of was his own perspective, this present moment. Frontier was so defined by the presence of the dam, by the holding of the water, how could it be moved? And because he couldn't understand or see beyond the present moment he had no hope in a change that would be the end of all he'd known, though the start of something new.

Eve was doing the dishes. Her mother and children were noisily clearing the table and moving about. Through the open door into the dining room she could just see the table and the men who were still sitting and talking. Dinner had been pleasant, and Eve knew it. Still at this moment she almost wished their little homestead wasn't connected to her parent's farm. That she and Josiah didn't work and meet here so often now that Mr. Bates was found here.

Josiah and John got along well with each other. The truth was beautiful to behold. It all seemed so natural that it tormented her.

She took another plate and washed off the remaining food. Why couldn't she wash off the remaining images of her visions as easily as the dried food? Around and around her thoughts and anger went, like the dishrag in her hand. But her only conclusion was that if she was wrong, if her thoughts were only that, rampant female thoughts, she, with God's help could cleanse them away. The fact that they remained after her prayers for help only convinced her further that they were from God. And His words, no matter how absurd they seem, would not be moved. She found herself irritated by the God she loved so dearly, because He had put her in this situation. Really, John Bates? Who is he? She prayed silently. She kept trying to reason away what was now unmasked before her. The harder she tried to think of a way out of this revelation the more her stomach turned and she had to take a few deep breathes to keep from vomiting. She felt relief, comfort , and a release from the fear of being alone, and as those thoughts blossomed in her she wanted to hate herself. Had God asked her to sit and quietly eat supper in the presence of the two men, who at different times in her life would both be her husband? She even knew He was trying to teach her something wonderful about the character of Christ, but the discomfort of the moment was keeping her from understanding the lesson.

She wanted to weep, but would not be able to offer any explanation for her tears. If all this was real and happening, then all she had seen was real and would happen. She had thought she had accepted losing Josiah the day she dug up that dead rose, but this was a new twist on an old pain. A new spice had been added to the recipe and she was struggling to swallow it. God's preparation for a new love was one thing, but to be made aware of it while still bound in a current marriage was quite another. She hadn't expected to witness these visions connect to the waking world in such a way until after God had done what He said He would. To be so accosted by the unseen, and out of time, once again caused her to question the goodness of God.

So was her internal turmoil that evening. On occasion she dropped a dish and the water splashed upon her face, no one ever entertained the thought that perhaps she had done so on purpose to hide the rebellious tear that had escaped her grasp.

The evening grew dark and the storm raged. The men spoke about Trevor Stanton and the dam and what was to be done. Blue Cloud gave insight to what his people may do and say about it all. The men grew tired long before any solution other than prayer could be found. John and Blue Cloud were offered to sleep in the bunk house and everyone agreed a good night's sleep was needed.

Blue Cloud was already bedded down for the night in the bunkhouse. John didn't want to disturb him so he tried to keep his movements quiet as he took off his boots and got ready to lie down. He felt strange, as if God had put him in a tiny box, and the walls were squeezing in around him, pushing him toward something that he believed he wanted and yet, because of what his eyes saw he doubted. He had always wanted to settle down in a place like this, and now he was wondering if this was perhaps the place. Everything seemed perfect, almost everything. His quiet thoughts were interrupted by Blue Cloud's voice.

"Lee believes you are one of Eve's dream people, John Bates." John looked up, although in the dimly lit shack he could see very little. He hadn't really caught what Blue Cloud had said and asked, "I'm sorry?"

Blue Cloud sat up and moved his blanket out of his way, and asked, "Did Lee tell you he believes you are one of Eve's dream people?" John was very tired and about ready to wash his hands of another cryptic conversation, yet replied, "I'm not sure I know what you mean?" Blue nodded and explained, "Eve sometimes sees people in her dreams, before she meets them in the waking world. Eve is what my people would call a Dream Walker, though not by her own design, the Creator calls her out." John pondered this. Perhaps that was what Lee had been referring to. Blue Cloud went on, "Eve is very close to her father, and she is close to me. Sometimes when her dreams are a burden she needs a safe place to share to talk through the visions that trouble her." Mr. Bates understood in part but needed a bit more information, "Why do they trouble her?" Blue Cloud shook his head, "Do you think speaking with the Creator would not be a troubling business." Mr. Bates had to chuckle a bit, "Well, I guess I see your point." Blue Cloud observed the other man with some interest. His coming had troubled Eve and he wondered at the depth of her revelation about him. Blue Cloud had his own suspicions that he chose to keep to himself for the time being. He took a slight turn to the conversation, "Why did you come here John Bates?"

John thought about how to answer, "Well, in truth, I've always wanted to see the West." Blue Cloud nodded. The hearts of men are woven by the Creator, the men themselves often not aware of the design that is put into them. They are simply content in one place or driven onto another. So it was with John.

John spoke next, his thoughts turning in another direction. "I hadn't really thought about what I would find in coming here, but the breaking of the dam, and meeting you, and the people here." Blue Cloud looked very hard at the man as John went on, "It feels like I just got here, and everything is about to change... is changing."

Blue Cloud looked at the flame of the lamp for a moment and sighed. He was thinking deeply, it was a hard matter to understand. "There are some things that are still a mystery John, but I will explain it as it was shown to me. This land is a great land, but it is broken, we as a people are broken, men like you are pieces that have been broken from other lands and placed here. Change is hard to accept, so the Creator sends lights among us, people whose stories can help us find our way to being a whole land and people again. Eve is one of these lights. He has sent a storm to rest over her head, and she wanted to run from the darkness it brought, but her eye was caught by a silver lining that shone around the edges of the cloud so lovely that she dared to stay and face the storm. You coming here, John Bates, has triggered something in Eve. I do not yet know if it is because you are a part of the cloud or the silver lining. I believe Eve knows and is shaken by it." Blue Cloud lay back down. He had nothing more to say at the moment.

There seemed to be nothing to say. Yet, he found an atmosphere, a presence, soothing and guiding that he could only attribute to someone like God and despite his own reservations about it, he had to consider that he was part of a vast design.

John lay back and drifted to sleep in sheer exhaustion. As he floated in that elusive realm, between consciousness and sleep, his soul had a moment of clarity. It passed before his mind could grasp it. John started out of his sleeplike state, thoughts and visions fading from memory as he woke. It took him a while to get back to sleep. His heart understood, for maybe the first time in his life, that he was exactly where he was supposed to be.

PART 9

Until the time that his word came:
the word of the Lord tried him. (j)

Oh these days of earthly bliss,
whither and fade 'neath heaven's kiss.
Onward, still to feel the pain,
yet grow new strength beneath the strain.
For heaven's love can bring new life,
and teach to be both widow and wife.

Eve was laughing as she let her arms fall from Josiah's shoulders and he stepped out the door. Placing his hat on his head he turned back and said, "See you tonight." Eve was waving and watched as one of the boys, seeing his dad heading off for the day, ran after him for a hug good bye.

It had been sometime since she had seen Mr. Bates. He had been away working up river surveying possible new locations for a future dam. She wondered about what he was doing from time to time, but had found great curiosity in the fact that she often saw him and Josiah together. Seeing the two of them side by side often pushed her to the limit of what she thought she could handle.

Summer had taken on another semblance of normalcy and Eve served and walked with her husband and children in true love that flowed from her broken yet beating heart.

Her dreams raged on and she kept her discipline of writing them down, and more than that, she had turned some into stories. That year proved eventful for Eve as one such story had been accepted for publication as a children's book.

The whole process of writing and painting had been hard, for she felt in part that she had worked to make her dreams become a reality, and there was an element of pain in that truth. God's love captivated her through the wounding, like a rose draws a hand through the thorns.

This story had come from a dream of wolves, often seen lurking in the bushes and woods of her nightly adventures. Salvation had come to her in the form of a large bear and it had carried her away to safety. The ending was both terrible and beautiful and through it Eve was able to see the self-sacrificing love of Christ in her circumstances.

The reality of being published birthed hope anew in the tiny household. Josiah was proud. He had always supported Eve's talents. The children as well begged and pleaded until Eve relented and came to the school to read her works.

In the midst of these sweet happenings Eve fell away into an unsanctified comfort and was chastened by a loving God.

The kids had spent the night at their grandparents and so Eve and Josiah found themselves alone in the kitchen that morning. Eve was cleaning up breakfast and Josiah was sipping his coffee looking out the window. The quiet house inspired him and he began to speak of the coming years when the children would be grown and moved out and it would just be the two of them. It had been some time since Eve had entertained such thoughts, her understanding having been directed toward a violent change of circumstances. It took only a moment, she pushed aside the years of work God had poured into her through Divine revelation and allowed herself to dream with Josiah that morning. They spoke of the house and garden, so many apparently normal and sweet ramblings that two people in love dare to entertain. As the conversation went on, though, Eve felt a tug within her, gentle at first, but it grew in intensity little by little.

Josiah smiled as he left for work as Eve shut the door and turned back to her daily duties but within an hour she was pressed over the sink in tears. The pain of turning her back on God, the loss of His grace upon her was more than she could bear. God's voice was resonating through her heart, "These are not the hopes I have for you." Her own feeble response, "But please, it was only a moment, just a glance at what might be." But God was firm, "I have told you it will not be. Why have you stepped away from me?" Eve grasped at her chest, the pain intense, "But I love him. How do I love him without the hope of a future with him?" God seemed to sigh at her, but it was much more than that, it was an intense blowing of displeasure, "Love is not bound in future expectation. You can enjoy life while under the certainty of death, child." Eve sat back in a chair. She knew it was true, but it wasn't easy. Oh, she was so frustrated with the difficulty of the path He was carving for her. She cried for some time from the pain before she was able to turn back onto the hard path of faith. It had been so many years of watching and waiting for God to do what He'd said. She had thought just one morning of hope, false as it was, couldn't hurt. But she had been wrong for hearts don't follow lightly. A glimmer of hope causes growth to burst abundantly in the landscape of a heart. God had worked long to change Eve's landscape and He wasn't about to let her plant anew what He had worked so hard to till down. He loved her too much for that. That path would only prolong her pain.

Eve heard her name and turned toward the sound. The hill sloped down in front of her and a presence, immense and sweet like her mother, called her down that hill. Eve heard a sound and turning saw a fire lit by one who was like her Lord. The flames grew and soon leapt onto her house. The orange and red stretched up gulping the air and raging into yellow and white fiery petals and shot out sparks toward the sky. The fire wrapped around the house and Eve ran after it toward the well in the back. As she ran she noticed the places of the house where the fire had already done its work, the outer siding was burnt off but a structure of steel was revealed and no internal damage was done. Still, Eve raced on, thinking of her children. They were still in that house!

At the well she filled the bucket, but it was undersized. Water in pathetic amounts splashed on the devouring blaze, squelching only a little. Despite her desperate efforts Eve could not put out the fire that burned but did not destroy her home. And still, that voice, loving and understanding was calling her down the hill.

The fire was dying down as Eve turned to do as the voice bid. Coming around the front of the house the front window was filled with light and Eve turned, fearful that an inferno had caught life within the house. But seeing through the front porch, which had not been damaged, into the window, she perceived another picture. Her children were sitting around a table with a man that was light itself, and His light filled the whole house and there was joy. Eve marveled at what she saw and hearing her name again she turned to go down the hill.

Instead of a stroll down the hill Eve stood looking down into a hole that led into a dark abyss. The man of light stood there, now wearing a body like a shade for his light. He was not handsome and yet Eve was drawn to him. He was telling her she needed to go down there, into that darkness. He held a rope by which he would let her down. Eve backed up, shaking her head, "No…no…" she stammered. She knew full well what was down in that darkness, it was ghastly, strange ghouls and beasts, terror and death lay down there, and worst of all she would lose sight of this man beside her in that darkness. Fear gripped her anew.

She turned and tried to reach for the light that was above, to go up the hill to the higher ground but she could not find a way and finally she stood again by the man with the rope. "You have to hold me!" she yelled at him, for wind and storm raged around. He looked at her and then down into the dark. She yelled again, "You have to hold me, do you understand, I can't do it unless you go with me!" He had smiled at her and stepping around the rope had held his hand out to her. Eve stepped into his embrace and her entire being was saturated with the most intense love she had ever known. So true and vehement was the experience of His love that she pulled away, out of sleep, God letting her for she had seen what she needed to.

Eve's eyes were open but she wasn't seeing the ceiling above her bed. She was seeing the dream, scene by scene, sometimes out of sequence as the more extreme encounters overwhelmed the order of their coming. Tilting her head back she closed her eyes. "I'm sorry God." She cried internally. And truly she was sorry, she had been resisting him every step of the way. What he was asking of her seemed simple, but the actuality of it beat against her natural proclivities every step of the way. Every human fiber of her being was constantly under assault by a loving God who tormented her by asking her to renew her mind. 'Leave your kids in the burning house, for I am the Burning. Go down into the dark, face you fears, for I am with you.'

Eve wondered about her fears, they seemed powerful despite the fact that they were only vapors. She had no idea what was really down the dark abyss of loss. She had witnessed others lose loved ones and deal with grief, but she really had no way to know for sure how the actual passing of God's will would affect her.

Thinking back she could remember the waves of grief that had accosted her when Josiah's mother had passed away. That was the closest loss she had experienced in her adult life. It had been a sad season, but she understood that grief was a process, a letting go, that passed in time. Now, although she missed Annie, she saw memories of her as joy…Eve wondered if she could come to such a place after losing her husband. She flung her covers back and sat up but didn't rise still thinking about all these things. Parts of her inner self, deep below the surface of daily function, knew that she would be alright. Still, her thoughts could only take her so far, as *experience can never be achieved in the preparation.*

Josiah and Eve were walking through the wild garden in the woods where he had proposed to her. Eve was enjoying his company. Josiah worked hard and returned home tired, afternoon walks together were a cherished escape for both of them.

The sunlight trickled down through the green canopy and crowned her lovely fingers as they were laced through his strong calloused ones. They had no agenda, each moment being defined by the view of the stream or the call of a small animal. Under the shelter of a drooping bow Josiah kissed her like he had done before they were married and Eve's heart overflowed with love. She truly loved him, and was happy in her life with him that fact had never changed. No matter how ardently God told her she was to lose him, she had never wanted to.

Crossing a small wooden bridge that had been made over the stream they stopped and watched the water fall over stones, the light catching the ripples and making them sparkle. Josiah put his arm around her waist and pulled her close to his side. Eve trembled in the moment and sighed. Enjoying the embrace and the beauty of their surrounding filled her eyes with tears. For she had achieved what He had been trying to teach her all along, what she had stumbled and struggled to do for so many years. She felt joy, and gratitude for her time, every moment she had with this man. Even if, by grand design, he was gone tomorrow, this day, this love…it was a gift and she had lived and held more such precious moments than she could ever number. God had been and was very good to her and she smiled away the tears and then laughed out loud, because this time, in this 'now'…they were tears of joy.

PART 10

The righteous perish and no man layeth it to heart... (k)

At Heaven's gate, are no good-bye's,
though loved ones left alone do cry.
Love is true and hope is more,
than what we need to walk that shore
No looking back on shadows dark,
for truer life turns coals to sparks.

The sun shone brightly as Josiah removed his hat to wipe the sweat from his face with his sleeve. Returning the stained leather rim he swung his pick axe into the stone again. Stanton had opened up the mine and men were working. Josiah was part of a crew high on the ridge, breaking a path up the mountain to what would soon be a new shaft.

It felt as if someone drew near. Josiah stopped working. The sensation was new and strange. He seemed to know someone was there, but it felt like more. It felt as if the sun itself had come out of the sky. The light increased until not a shadow could be seen anywhere. Josiah turned. And his face was filled with the purest and sweetest recognition.

I could say much about the next few months and how the actuality of Josiah's death affected those who knew him, but I will choose to say little. Eve was not the only person to mourn him. She had simply been mourning longer.

God blessed them, and Josiah's wife and children not only lived on, but continued to live well. That's not to say there weren't dark days or many tears, there were, but the sun always shone brighter after the night and the tears that fell watered the seeds God had planted and new hopes began to sprout.

The dam, along with everything else in Frontier, seemed locked in time as winter tightened her icy embrace once again. By the light of a warm fire Trevor Stanton met with town council members, one by one showing them plans and speaking to them of the future of Frontier as he poured them his best brandy.

It was evening, the sun just beginning to rest on the hills. The days were getting warmer and the snow was melting everywhere. Eve hadn't as yet been noticed on the porch of Miss Ruth's. Her approach for some reason had been unheard, so she was pacing lightly across the wooden planks. Her fingers were trying to grind up the book in her hands. Words she had written and sealed up, before...before she could have known, unless God alone had told her. And she had buried it, in a way, out of sight. Now the present reality had made it true but Eve was struggling with sharing it. As if by her own strength she could undo the work God had done in her over the past years. But no matter how she bent and rubbed, the words remained in her hands as her leather bound journal and her heart faltered.

Fear and doubt tried to have their way but a change had occurred in Eve. She could feel it, no longer buried deep but now just beneath the surface. All she had to do was reach for it. Could it be that simple? All she had to do was share her journey and ask a question.

She knew she was being asked to do a very easy and natural thing. Through the years she had hoped and prayed for the coming of this day. Then it had been a glorious hope, a reason to go on. Now, she trembled at reality of it. But that was what He had changed in her through the long process. Eve had endured truth. That was the name of it Truth. For good or for bad she had heard the truth from the original author. She had been tried by time as she waited to see what she had heard. There is no way to explain the intricate adjustment that does to a person's soul, to their mind. The very fabric of her being was now altered. She had endured her sorrow at His bidding. She dared not step back when all she had to do was reach out and claim rest. The promise was the only reason she had endured the pain. The pain had come. Her resolve to claim the promise blossomed into a boldness she had not yet known.

Her diary contained the truth about her 'knowing.' She had written of how God's words had entered her heart and divided it in two. She had seen herself giving her diary to her second love more than once and still she felt unprepared. She prayed that she had walked through this well, doing well before God, still now she stood having to take one last great step and it wasn't easy.

It should have been easy. Wasn't this what she had been waiting for? To somehow have the ability to tell John that she loved him, that God had been guiding them toward each other? She had seen too much to doubt God, doubt what He told her, but she doubted herself, her own understandings. What if Mr. Bates wasn't the man from her dreams, but a man 'like' him, what if he was just a forerunner that first friend who stirs the heart but isn't the one to stay?

The lace curtain barely moved beneath Miss Ruth's gentle touch. Her dark eyes brimmed with tears as she looked down on her friend pacing across her front porch. "Oh, Lord, give her strength to do her part. Cause you know Lord, that I'm gonna do mine." Miss Ruth made her way down the stairs and was happy to see Mr. Bates coming out of the kitchen toward the stairs. She leaned gently on the banister and waved at him. "Good, there you are." She came down the rest of the way and motioned to the door. "It's for you." John raised his eyebrows in question to what she was talking about. Miss Ruth tucked her chin and gave him a slight push toward the door as she walked by into the kitchen. "Sweet Jesus, give me patience…answer the door Mister, she's here for you." And with that she disappeared out of the hallway and John opened the door wondering how he could have missed hearing a knock.

Light fell all around her and Eve realized the door had opened and a very surprised Mr. Bates stood before her. "Well, hello Eve. I'm sorry I didn't realize you were here." He looked up and out into the rain that was beginning to fall. He turned a bit and asked, "Would you like to come in." Eve didn't want him to call Miss Ruth to persuade her. She answered abruptly, "No!" and Mr. Bates was puzzled, as he realized she didn't intend to come in the house, even with the threat of the rain. Eve smiled and tried to shake herself into steadiness. "Actually, I came here to see you." Mr. Bates tried to hide it, but the truth was he was pleased to hear her say it. He said nothing but stood and allowed himself to look squarely at her. Eve lowered her gaze to what she held in her hands. "I need to give this to you." She said and dared to look up. He was open and waiting, undisturbed by her actions. Eve looked down and rambled on a bit, "I'm sorry, I'm a bit nervous." Mr. Bate smiled gently at her. He had been hoping for such a moment. Could it be that her grief had passed? He had been wrestling for months with how to show a grieving woman just how much he cared.

Eve was at the end of her sight when it came to what his reading her words might do to them. All she knew was that she had to give it to him...so with trembling hands she passed it into his. "This is, well it's my diary. But I feel as if I'm supposed to let you know more of what I went through, or am going through." She was flustered, "It's hard to explain." Mr. Bates took the book and looked up at her. Grief was a strange beast, haunting each person in a different form. He wondered what Eve's was like.

She imagined a hundred different things she could have said at that moment, but no words could ever do justice to the depths of what she knew and felt. So she dared to look into his eyes and in them there was a glimmer of something that gave her hope causing her to smile slightly. She managed to say, "I guess it's my way of asking you a question." Mr. Bates returned her gaze. Eve shrugged her shoulders, how could there be so few words. Still she went on, "You've been a good friend to me and my family through a difficult time and I want to thank you for that. I know that you haven't found a solution Stanton is happy with so there might not be much reason for you to stay around here much longer." Mr. Bates felt his whole countenance drop. Such things had been heavy on his mind as well lately. Eve felt a courage she didn't know she possessed well up and she spoke directly, "Well, the truth is that I...want you to understand so that you will still think well of me." She was slowly moving closer as she spoke. "Because it may not yet…seem proper for me to tell you that I love you." Eve had finally said it out loud. The release was intoxicating and she found she could smile as she drew back off the porch.

Mr. Bates watched her get on her horse and gallop off. He stood in the door elated but in no way aware of what was contained in the journal he held in his hands.

The spring storms stood back and let the sun through on the day that Miss Maybelle Campbell was marrying Jimmy Jackson, who happened to be Tommy's little brother. It seemed like the whole town had shown up for the celebration. Eve had been up early, spending the day with her mother preparing and decorating the little chapel for the wedding. Lee and a small band of young men from the Jackson clan finished up the dance floor out back.

She was trying to keep her hands busy. In hopes that using her fingers to set flowers would stop her mind from wondering if Mr. Bates would be there tonight, or calm the fluttering in her stomach such thoughts evoked.

Lee performed a short, but lovely wedding as the two young people were surrounded by friends and family who shared their joy. The afternoon service was followed by a warm wind that filled the valley and everything seemed to be in order for a good time that would last well into the night.

Eve had seen Mr. Bates from a distance but he hadn't sought her out so she resolved to think the worst, that she was now a lunatic he would avoid her at all cost. It was a comforting thought, for it was a better alternative than supposing that he simply felt nothing for her.

Eve found herself walking behind the food tables and the gift table, gazing toward the sunset, her thoughts dark and her mood broody. She could see so many people, in fact the entire town about to be faced with a great loss, yet unwilling to acknowledge it, just as she had been for such a long time. She didn't want to feel sad at the moment. This didn't seem like the right time or place. But there were too many reminders today. Despite her ability to cope with her grief and the distraction of Mr. Bates, she was thinking of her own wedding day.

The colors of the distant sunset caught her eye and her heart was touched with the memory of Josiah. She simply missed him so much at times. She bowed her head and wondered, how much of her loneliness was actually in missing Josiah in particular and how much was just missing having a husband. Despite the fact that Josiah was gone, she was still conflicted by the feelings Mr. Bates had woken up within her. The rainbow light on the horizon reminded her of a future wedding she had seen in the land of sleep. She then found herself listing all the reasons why it couldn't be Mr. Bates. Perhaps he wasn't going to stay in Frontier. She had three children and so on. Yet, there were things she couldn't argue away. Like the way he looked at her and it gave her cause to consider. She felt free to love but she was still haunted by doubt.

The light of the sunset changed ever so slightly while a flicker of the divine brushed against her causing her to remember what had slipped out of her Bible that morning and fallen to the floor. It was a folded piece of paper, a page from her journal that she had torn out, folded, and kept tucked within her Bible's pages. Words she had written so many years before had appeared like new acquaintances rather than forgotten sorrow. It was a dream, but not one of hers. She had recorded a dream Josiah had shared with her. It had been at a time when she had been refusing to believe that God was telling her he was going to call Josiah home.

On that distant morning, Eve woke to the sound of Josiah taking in a deep inhale of air, almost a backward shriek. Eve rolled over to see Josiah blinking determinedly as if trying to focus on something he could not see with his eyes. "I just had the strangest dream." He said. It was an interesting occurrence for Josiah rarely dreamt.

The sun was already up and peeking in the windows. Eve turned on her side, facing him and got comfortably situated in her pillows. She was still sleepy and thought she could shut her eyes while he told her about it. Josiah spoke again without being asked, "I was here. I was looking out the windows." Eve opened her eyes and looked at him. That was notable; windows in a dream were symbolic of being given sight, ability to see out of the world around you, even into heaven at times. Josiah was lying on his back and motioning with his hands as he spoke, as if trying to form what he had seen. "And you came, and you told me that what I was seeing, what was outside the windows, were only paintings and that it wasn't real. There were higher, truer windows, above." He turned his head toward the window in their room, as if expecting to see something other than the morning light in the pine trees outside. "I looked out the higher windows, and I saw the ocean." His eyes opened wide as he thought of the ocean being just outside. But then he closed his eyes and he continued as if seeing the present window was conflicting with his memory and he wanted to relate it correctly. "There was a type of sandbar, like a path out into the ocean and I was walking out onto the water." He shook his head gently, "I didn't want to go, but the further I went, the more beautiful it became. It was so beautiful! The water was crystal blue, so clear I couldn't believe it." He dropped his hands and opened his eyes as he finally stated, "And finally it was just so beautiful that I wanted to go."

Eve had no words. They both lay there for a long time. Each considering the dream, but unwilling to speak what they were thinking. Eve could tell that the dream was both wonderful and upsetting to Josiah. Eve reached out and he took her hand and held it upon his chest, but neither one of them ever spoke of it.

Eve suppressed a sob as grief and joy cascaded through her. The beauty of a God and a heaven that were beyond all the enticements of this mortal world overcame her sadness. A man she loved in such a precious way was gone, but not dead.

Eve stood, in the aftermath of God's will. She shuddered as other memories of dreams swirled around in her head. Like Josiah she now stood on the brink of another chapter in her life, she wondered what kind of beauty would entice her to step out into it when all she wanted to do was hide back in the comfort of her seemingly insignificant existence.

A happy tune rang out from the banjo, soon followed by the rest of the band and Eve turned and watched a few people begin dancing. 'Thank you, God' she prayed softly. Though the town was full of so much tension and fear as the spring rains had swelled the river higher than anyone could remember; she hoped a night of fun would be a soothing balm.

Miss Ruth came and wrapped an arm around Eve's waist, "You alright, girl?" she asked and Eve leaned over into the friendly embrace. Miss Ruth looked at her and shook her head, "It'll be alright, God has a plan. He's gonna take care of all of us. You'll see. You ain't gonna get asked to dance hiding over here, child." Eve shook her head, "I'm afraid I'm not really in the mood for dancing." And Eve turned her gaze back to the distant horizon as Miss Ruth stepped away, shaking her head. Eve wasn't the type of girl to go begging for a partner, but she shouldn't be hiding out! This wasn't a time for Eve to be carrying the weight of the world on her shoulders.

Now Miss Ruth had never seemed to be able to find a bush to beat around. She walked decidedly around the band and seeing a group of young men standing around talking rather than getting out on the dance floor, she headed for them like a hound into a flock of wild turkeys. Her boisterous reprimands soon sent them all flying in search of a partner. She noticed Mr. Bates gazing into the crowd, as if looking for someone.

"Go on, with you, your gal is over that way, behind them tables." She motioned in the direction she had just come from. Mr. Bates allowed himself to give her a questioning look and was soon accosted with, "Now don't you act like you don't know what I'm talking about, here, Mr. John Bates, I got eyes! You get over there and ask that woman to dance or you won't get no breakfast come morning." She turned and walked away, continuing her reprimands and threats in comical undertones. Mr. Bates headed in the direction she had pointed, and just as he had suspected, he saw Eve standing, arms folding in front of her, watching, but not partaking of the celebration herself.

"Why aren't you dancing, Eve?" He asked as he stepped up just behind her. The realization that someone had drawn near to her so unexpectedly startled Eve for a moment. Her surprise was soon replaced by what felt like a million butterfly's fluttering inside her, as she recognized the voice. She turned back to the dance floor shaking her head, trying to find something to say, but she could truly think of nothing so he dared to take her by the hand and lead her out into the swirling mob.

Eve's sadness seemed completely forgotten somewhere in between the festive music and Mr. Bates smiling eyes. He was a lively dancer and Eve was soon laughing in enjoyment. Tommy broke out in the center of the dance floor, alone, causing cheers to ring out. His brother, the groom, joined him and the two put on quite a show. Tommy spun and stomped a final step in front of Mr. Bates, an obvious invitation to join them. To Eve's surprise, Mr. Bates left her side as he and Tommy danced circles around each other. Others stepped up to show off their footwork as well. Mr. Bates remembered his partner, and returned to take her in his arms to swirl around the dance floor again. Eve was having a good time, Mr. Bates wondered how long it had been since she had smiled like that.

The music died down for a moment and a slower more melodic tune began. Mr. Bates did not let go of his hold on her, he simply slowed their dance down in time with the music. They danced in silence for a minute or two save for that unspoken communication that passes between a man and a woman when they find themselves in each other's arms.

Mr. Bates found himself wondering greatly at the woman before him. He was curious if it was possible that she could be in love with a man from her dreams. Her journal had given him a glimpse of her struggles but there was still much he didn't understand.

"Tell me about dream walkers, Eve." She looked up and blinked at the question.

He raised his eyebrows and she smiled faintly relieved to be able to speak about a generic topic, she wondered if he had read her journal and if he had understood what she meant in giving it to him, but she said, "Well, the Natives call someone who can walk in and out of others dreams a dream walker. " Eve took a breath and dared to look in his eyes, "I never sought it. I mean, I never asked for my dreams. When I was young sometimes God would answer my prayers in a dream. I read in the Bible of God doing that. Conversations with God and angels often occurred in dreams. I never thought it was strange. Until my dreams became a flood and I would see things before they happened sometimes and people…before I had met them."

He responded, "Am I one of those people Eve?"

Eve took a deep breath, she wasn't sure she really wanted to allow this turn in the conversation. Here and now in the middle of all these people. The song ended and another melody began and Eve let herself be carried away by Mr. Bates blue eyes.

"Yes. I can't explain more because I don't know more. The Bible says God gives us dreams to seal our instruction. I've had too many dreams come true to not…pay attention when something coincides in real life. And it's more than what I see, what I feel is real…it's" Mr. Bates finished her sentence for her when she stalled, "…love?"

Eve stiffened and became very aware of the strength of his shoulders and the closeness of his breathing. She felt as if the world was closing in around her and she stood on a pinhead of accumulating circumstances, a pivotal moment. What she knew to be true could not be shaken no matter how ridiculous it may appear to another. His face was near hers and she let her eyes examine him closely, he was so new and yet so familiar. His jaw line was showing a slight shadow of coming beard, his dark hair lay softly across his brow and his eyes, those eyes. Were those the eyes she had seen in her dreams so many times, or where they merely like them. Had she seen him in her dreams because the man that would come would be similar or like him, or was it actually him?

Seeing things in life that she had first seen in dreams happened often enough to her that she was no longer surprised by it, yet, she had thought she would feel more certainty. Especially when so many memories encased her consciousness to such an extent that she couldn't tell if she was awake or dreaming for a moment.

Her spirit and her heart had leapt of a cliff, singing, "We know, we know!" and she found herself scared that at the last minute the landscape would change revealing not a leap but another leg in a long journey. But the strings that attached her reasoning mind to her deeper feelings were too strong and surely set and she dared to believe. Just as she could not 'unknow' anything God had set for her to know, she could not help but feel those things He had placed in her to feel. In this her heart was settled; she loved him. Now she was only waiting to know what he was feeling.

Eve looked away and answered, "I've seen many men in my dreams, Mr. Bates. Often God shows himself as my father or even mother, or a trusted friend like Blue Cloud. And there are times when it is in waking that an image from a dream becomes potent, when you meet someone and you can't get over an impression, a knowing." Eve stopped herself before she said anything more, finding herself locked in his gaze, the feel of her hand in his, the height of his shoulder under her hand, the feel of his breath on the side of her face, even his scent. All of these things were realities flooding her mind woven in memories beyond counting. She had to focus very hard to keep her feet under her. Shaking her head she felt she babbled on, "The way we see other people what we call our relationship to them is often defined by our circumstances at the time of our meeting. I believe God can preset our perceptions if He chooses to." Eve hoped he was beginning to understand her struggle. Not only with the loss of Josiah, but with never being able to see him as a 'friend' or 'brother' as she felt she should have. Almost from the earliest moment of meeting him she had 'seen' him as husband. Now she waited for his answer to her question. Was this 'vision' of him true? Or was she to wait for another?

Mr. Bates was captivated by her words and the feel of her in his arms. "It makes you wonder at a Divine plan, things that are meant to be?" Eve nodded but looked away.

"May I ask how long it's been, Eve?" Eve lifted her face toward his, and shook her head slightly and replied, "What ..?" Mr. Bates smiled, "I mean, since you knew about... I'm sure a day like today…" Eve nodded and dared to look into his eyes. "It's been many years just over ten I think, since I understood He was going to take him." she said. Mr. Bates continued, "It's alright to say his name." Eve took in a breath and held it. She nodded as she looked into the crowd of dancing people. It was a wonderful sensation to know that he had known Josiah. He had seen her loss and was willing to join her where she was. It was a comfort she had not expected and it enabled her to look up and say, "Josiah."

Mr. Bate smiled a sweet intimate smile, and then, he kissed her.

Everything changed for Eve then. For the first time, she allowed herself to be comforted. She had kept those Divinely planted seeds of promise tucked away in a locked box. She whirled as his kiss unhinged the box and she experienced the fullness of a love that can only be known after sorrow

PART II

He taketh away the first,
that he may establish the second. (1)

Rain falls down, to tell of tears
Thunder breaks, speaking of fears
Light your fires, kindle your flames
For cold and calculated sin remains.

Eve's lips parted from Mr. Bates' as a light rain began to fall. The cool water changed the atmosphere of the party causing people to groan in disappointment. Tommy hopped onto the stage, made a quick toast to the bride and groom and said thanks so the guests would be released to head home.

Eve stood looking at Mr. Bates in a fluster of what to do now. The rain had a cooling effect on their embrace. "I'd better see to the kids." She said looking up into the thick clouds. It wasn't quite dark out the distant sunset could still be seen shining beneath the gathering storm.

Before Mr. Bates could reply, they heard sound of galloping hooves as a man rode into the dispersing crowd. The animal had run hard under the weight of a large man. Mr. Brown pulled his horse around, looking through the crowd. He called out, "Lee! I'm looking for Lee Wood! Mr. Bates! Is Mr. Bates here?" Mr. Bates being nearer stepped up and Lee called out from the front of the chapel. Mr. Brown went on for all to hear, "Mr. Stanton's holding a town meeting." He stated, as if that alone should rouse interest. Someone in the crowd asked, "What now, during the wedding? Half the town's here." Mr. Brown tried to look through the rain and find the speaker, but the shower was slowly and steadily growing in intensity. Lee stepped up beside Mr. Bates. Mr. Brown, seeing the men he had come for, continued his report. "He's calling for votes on the town lot commission." Lee looked to Mr. Bates, angered by what he now saw as Stanton's plan. Lee guessed, "He's planning to take control of the property rights. Those who don't want to head to the mountains will have to buy the higher lots from him to rebuild." Mr. Brown shook his head, "It's worse than that Lee, he's trying to sell the town, all his businesses, everything. He'll likely get everything the town has in the treasury."

Brian Cuthright stepped up beside Lee, along with many others, who were now interested in what was being said. Mr. Brown nodded at Lee, "The meetings starting in twenty minutes. If we hurry and get enough of us there..." Lee turned and called out, "Let's go." and immediately people went into motion. Many grabbed horses and headed out, while others, like Lee, needed to borrow a horse for their wagons were full of wives and kids who needed to get home out of the rain.

Eve rode up, leading two horses she had procured for her dad and Mr. Bates. She called to them and Mr. Bates turned in surprise, he hadn't even realized she had left his side. Lee swung up on the horse, "Your mom's headed home with the kids?" Eve gave him a nod and a look that dared him to tell her to go home with them. He nodded in understanding and turning his horse kicked him into high gear while Eve and Mr. Bates followed suit.

Mr. Trevor Stanton's eloquence was in fine form as he spun a story about wanting to head north in search of more mining opportunities. The engineer he had hired believed the mine should be abandoned, and he hoped to start a new chapter in his life. He was ready to move out of his father's shadow and make his own way. He had devised a plan, and already sold two of his saloon's and the hotel, yet he owned well over a hundred acres of what was now pasture land and he wanted to sell it to the town, for future building as the town grew.

Stanton introduced Miss Swanson as his fiancé using his coming nuptials to misdirect the peoples focus away from his hiring of an engineer and the decline of the mine.

At first Mr. Stanton didn't notice the few wet wedding guests who trickled in. He needed a majority vote to pass his proposal that the town buy the land. He knew what the town funds were and he carried on about his urgency to head out along with his willingness to sell the land at a price the town could afford. It seemed like a great offer to the trustee board who were about to pass a vote in favor, when Lee Wood stepped in the door. Removing his dripping hat he immediately made a motion, with respect, to make a statement to the town council before they made their decision.

Trevor Stanton's face went stone cold. Lee Wood stood his ground, acting as the wedge that would separate Stanton from his goal. He was caught in a trap of his own making and stood there in solemn resolve as he decided to hold his ground as long as he could. He stepped over to Miss Swanson and had her escorted home as the rain was coming down. She was a bit alarmed by her sudden departure but it passed for she was contented with her future prospects and his apparent affection. The slight pause turned the atmosphere in the room.

Lee walked up to the front and took his place facing the small but influential crowd. He knew most of them by name, they all knew him to be honest and respectable. Lee knew himself well enough to buy a few moments to grow comfortable in the situation and pray God would give him the right words to say. He started out casually and watched as Mr. Bates and Eve entered along with half a dozen or more filing in from the wedding behind them.

"I apologize for my late arrival," he began and gave a pointed look at Mr. Stanton as he continued, "but we were having a wedding, and I was only just informed of this meeting, so please forgive me for not being more prepared."

Trevor shifted uneasily as he eyed Mr. Bates and others in the crowd. Lee spoke on, "It's come to my attention that there are certain details with regard to the future of this town that you may not be aware of.

Now I don't know what Mr. Stanton has told you, but the engineer that he hired," and he motioned toward Mr. Bates, "has come to the conclusion that our dam is likely to fail," Lee lifted his voice as he continued to speak over the many exclamations and exchanges that began to occur, "and he suggests that we relocate the town to higher ground." The whole room filled with raised voices and unintelligible distress.

Mr. Stanton decided to act as if he was only just hearing of this himself. "Let's settle down, everyone, settle down. Obviously, I was not aware that Mr. Bates had any such ideas. My interest in all this has been to get my mine up and running. If Mr. Bates has some new information about the integrity of the dam, then let's hear it." He lifted his arm in an inviting gesture and Mr. Bates rose and joined them in the front.

Mr. Bates rose to the occasion, "I know many of you have questions, but what Lee had said is true. It is my professional opinion that the river is going to breach the dam."

Questions began ringing out, "When?" "How long do we have?" Mr. Bates waited respectfully until the voices died down enough that his answers could be heard. Mr. Stanton stood with a smug expression on his face. John dipped his head in angry admission that this alarming news would be watered down by inability to accurately predict how much time the dam had. He tried, "It's difficult to know when. Often in such situations as this a dam will be intentionally blown, but in light of the fact that the town has been built in the rivers path, your best option is to post watches, have a flood alarm, and begin to relocate as soon as possible."

The unease of the crowd grew in turbulence and Stanton gave Sheriff Long a nod. The Sheriff, a close friend of Mr. Stanton stood and called for attention. "Now let's not let everybody fly into a panic. The man said, 'it's difficult to know when the dam might break. We've got to keep our heads cool, and deal with this properly and decidedly."

That was when Miss Ruth walked through the doors. At that moment, many people were at a loss for words anyway, and the sight of Miss Ruth, soaked wet with rain water, striding through the crowd as if she was showing off her new Sunday hat, made the crowds loss for words a decided fact. She marched straight up front and took a seat. Eve stood in the back of the room and had to smile at the audacity of her dear friend.

Lee was the first to break the silence. "I think we should make a motion to close the meeting, that no town funds be used," and he glanced at Stanton, "until we have prayerfully and thoughtfully considered the matter of the dam, and that a committee be chosen to begin plans for temporary houses on higher ground."

Miss Ruth was heard loud and clear above the clamor of the crowd, with an, "Amen!"

Stanton, however, would not accept defeat, "Well, now you can't put a hold on people selling their land, if they decide they would rather sell out than 'relocate' that is their choice."

Mr. Bates had just about lost his patience with Trevor Stanton. The crowd began to holler their agreement with the statement. Lee managed to calm them down. Mr. Bates spoke, "Mr. Wood is not saying you can't sell out, all we're saying is that the town should probably not invest all of its funds in land that will soon be under water."

Stanton was sweating, and flicked his fingers in irritation by his side. Mr. Bates continued, "I have made a full report, and I suggest you reconvene in a day or two and consider what I have to say about the dam."

A man stood in the crowd and asked, "I thought you were going to fix the dam."

Mr. Bates spoke in reply, "I do not believe it can be fixed, the problem is too deep, and there may not be enough time to construct a new one before it will fail."

The people began to murmur, the atmosphere of fear and unrest growing. No one had seemed to notice, but Eve had moved around and was standing at the edge of the platform near her father. People were beginning to grow very uneasy, asking each other what they should do, if they should leave, is our house in danger and so on.

Someone called out, "But a new dam could be made?"

Mr. Bates nodded, "Yes, but you would be taking a great risk if you remained downstream as it was being built. In cases as this people usually blow the dam rather than wait for the inevitable, but with so many lives at stake we need to get people moving to higher ground."

Lee noticing his daughter, sighed, and waited again for the murmurs to ebb down so that he could speak.

When all eyes were on Lee he took a breath and nodded. "Excuse me, but I think we need to remember, that although this news may seem like a surprise to us, God has always known this day was going to come. That water has already claimed lives, my daughter didn't want to lose her husband, but she did. We don't want to change our ways, but we're going to have to. God is going to give us all we need to get through it. We love this place, and we've invested in this town, but if we want to move on, we're going to have to take a turn we didn't see coming. He's giving us fair warning, I hope, so we don't need to be afraid, but ask God for the courage to say good bye to Frontier as we've known it, and make us ready to embrace the new place He has for us." His words seemed to hang like a calming fog over the crowd.

One of the trustees, a portly man with spectacles, that Lee vaguely recognized, stood and cleared his throat. "In light of this news, I'm sorry Mr. Stanton, but I don't believe it would be in the town's best interest to purchase your land at this time. I move to close the meeting and reconvene, tomorrow, to discuss Mr. Bates plans for relocating." His motion was seconded and Mr. Stanton could do nothing but stew in his own anxieties as he watched the town members begin to file out of the building.

Stanton's eyes were glistening and his jaw was constantly clenching and unclenching. He pulled out his watch and looked at it, not because he desired to know the time, but it was a familiar practice of his and soothed him. Long asked, "Is there anything we can do?" Stanton shook his head, "Not really."

The meeting broke up and the room emptied as everyone made their way out. Mr. Bates found himself in the middle of the room, following Lee as Lee was speaking to Eve and Miss Ruth, when he saw Stanton standing between them and the door fiddling with his watch. Mr. Bates hoped they could pass by, but Mr. Stanton grabbed Eve by the arm as she passed and turned her toward him.

"Don't pin all your hopes on him, Eve." Eve was surprised to be so taken by Mr. Stanton, but she wasn't afraid, "We should all put our hopes in God, Mr. Stanton." She said plainly. He chuckled softly and pulled her closer and whispered hoarsely, "I'm not talking about God, Eve." He said and relaxed his hold on her as Lee and Mr. Bates stepped up, concerned by Stanton's actions. Stanton let go of Eve, who was still looking at him, wondering if he was going to explain his comment more. Stanton lifted his hat to his head and smiled his charming smile as he continued loud and clear, "I'm talking about our dear Mr. Bates here. I understand he's been making arrangements to start his journey back to England. He's booked passage on the stage that comes first of next month." He turned his head toward Bates with a slight shake of his head, as if to say, oh my, you hadn't told them yet. Stanton turned away from Bates, who was seething in anger, and continued speaking to Eve, "He's not going to stick around Eve," and he blinked, "not even for you."

Eve stood in shock, she was exhausted and her mind struggled to process everything she had just heard. Lee laid his hands over Eve's shoulders, "Let's go Eve, we can talk about it later." Lee's eyes bore into Stanton, letting him know that Stanton had done his worse and could have nothing more to say. Stanton smiled softly as they moved out the door onto the covered walkway.

Stanton sidled up beside Bates as he moved to follow his friends. Bates was perplexed by how Stanton had known, and enraged with what he had done with the information. What shred of hope he had held onto, had seemed to shatter as he saw the news break upon Eve's unsuspecting face.

Mr. Stanton pulled out a cigar and began lighting it. He was reveling in his small victory and choosing to ignore that he had just been out done by Bates in regard to the town. He began speaking, "I have to say, I'm disappointed for you Mr. Bates." Bates turned in utter disbelief that this man was going to try to irritate him further. Stanton continued, nodding up the valley, "You didn't fix the dam, you're not going to get paid," Stanton took a puff on his cigar and pulled it away flicking the embers as he continued, "and you're not going to get the girl." He put his matchbox back in his pocket, puffing his chest up as he did it. He smiled and lifting his cigar up to his lips, the fiery embers glowing bright and orange in the dark, he continued, "I guess it is time for you to tuck tail, and head back…"

Bates wasn't aware he hit Stanton until he saw the cigar's orange sparks spiraling into the rain. Stanton stepped to the side, doubled over, with a hand to his mouth, but before he could even notice the blood that was pooling in his palm he plunged head first into Mr. Bates side and the two of them flew off the porch and out into the muddy street.

Sherriff Long stepped out onto the porch his hand on his gun but Lee was faster than Long expected and laid his hand over Long's, locking his gun in the holster until Lee saw fit to let it go, or take the gun.

The icy rain and heavy mud could not cool the rage of the two men and Stanton stood, spitting blood and grinning. The mouthful of red teeth spurred Bates' rage on and he charged at

Stanton. They tumbled in an indiscernible tangle and when they parted, Stanton lay stunned. Mr. Bates picked himself up and stood over Stanton as Stanton came to his senses. Bates grabbed him by his jacket and lifting him up shouted, "You're a small greedy man Stanton! You haven't a thought but how to line your own bloody pockets!" Then he let Stanton fall into the mud that was threatening to consume him and Mr. Bates spoke with less intensity, "You're so afraid of what you'll lose, you can't see what you'll gain." Stanton looked up in disbelief and Bates stepped away. Stanton soon found that he was indeed bogged down in the mud and couldn't move, much like a turtle on its back.

Eve watched in silence as Mr. Bates made his way back to the cover of the porch. He had a small cut over one eye, but most of his injuries were concentrated on his hands. He was wet and miserable, his rage dying away into despair.

Lee knew they all needed a break and a good night's sleep. Stanton began hollering for Long and Lee pulled out Long's pistol and released the ammo into the ground before replacing the gun in the holster. Lee spoke as he dropped each bullet, "I think" plink, "that you should" plunk, "be spending your time" plink, plunk, "looking for the men" plunk, thunk, "who tried to kill my daughter and that engineer, rather than being Stanton's guard dog, Long." Long glanced toward Stanton then back to Lee, he seemed unsure of how to proceed. Stanton had been his safe bet in this town and he stood in shock of seeing him beaten by this strange new comer. Stanton bellowed again for Long's assistance and Lee stepped back so Long could retrieve his boss. Lee dared to tell the Sherriff "Now you make sure he doesn't do anything stupid, Long." Long stopped and almost turned to look back, but then walked on. He was a dark cruel man, but with Stanton losing control of the town Lee hoped Long would leave. Lee then encouraged Miss Ruth to take Mr. Bates home and tend to his wounds while he shepherded his daughter along as well.

I thought you showed me, so clearly,
all these things before
But now the vision's clouded,
and you seem to've shut the door
I thought I could see the whole picture,
from the piece, very small I could see
But I'll learn that you've shown but a glimpse, of all
that you have planned for me.

Eve opened her eyes as the morning sunlight invaded her room despite the protest of a heavy curtain. She squinted and stretched, she was sore and as she stepped, bit by bit into wakefulness, memories flooded her consciousness. At first she thought it was a dream, a horrible strange dream, but when she noticed her wet and muddy clothes on the floor, the reality of the night before was made very clear.

Eve dressed and found her way down stairs. The intensity of the night before and thoughts of now heading home and tending to her own little farm steered her thoughts away from Mr. Bates for a few minutes. It was Saturday and her mother was feeding the kids a late breakfast. Betty smiled softly at her daughter and kissed her cheek good morning. But Eve was distracted, she didn't know how to feel or think about anything at the moment. In truth she wanted to just sit right down and cry, but the rumbling in her stomach and the smiles of her children attempted to overthrow her heartache, for the time being.

Betty watched her daughter eat and sipped her tea. Lee had filled her in on much of what had happened, and although Eve had no way of knowing, her mother knew much more about Eve's present distress than Eve would have guessed.

Eve lay her fork down and was gazing out the window toward the sheds wondering where her father was. The disappointment from last night overcrowded all other thoughts. Every fiber of her being was wondering about Mr. Bates. She didn't want to believe he was just going to leave, when it seemed that they needed him the most. She stopped herself, it was more than that. She actually wanted him with a love and desire that overwhelmed her own experiences and expectations of such feelings. She had hoped in him, and now everything seemed to be set to quench the light of that hope. She felt like a fool, "Dear God, why did you lead me here?" she wondered.

Betty noticed the sad look on her daughter and ushered the kids into the kitchen, yet again, to do dishes. She combated their grumpy protests with stern instruction and a promise that they could help her make cookies once they had the dishes done.

Betty then took her tea and sat beside her daughter. Eve noticed her mother's presence and leaned into her shoulder. Eve teared up, "Oh, mom... Why? Why did God open up my feelings... I've tried so hard to guard my heart...Why would he do this?" Betty wrapped an arm around her daughter, "Oh, honey, calm down, you don't have the whole picture yet, only God does." Eve looked up at this, "What do you mean?" Betty hugged her closer and then let her go, "I mean nothing God has promised you has changed, nothing you have come to know and believe has faltered in any way that you should lose heart."

Eve didn't know how to respond. Of course it had! Mr. Bates was leaving. If he was the one she was to marry, that she had been waiting for, what was all this, just another turn of a page to reveal yet another season of waiting to gain another understanding?

Betty poured a bit more tea and went on, "You know honey, I've always wondered why you didn't leave this little place, before you married Josiah. I know you felt I was disappointed in you marrying and staying here, but it wasn't really that, it's just…" She turned to her daughter and brushed a strand of hair from her face, "You're so full of spark, and light. You're smart and creative in a way that seemed to be destined for more than this little town. Your sisters have married and settled, and though I know you're very attached to us, and this place, I hope that you find the courage to go out and do all God has for you to do. I see now that God was just tucking you away here, until it was His perfect time." Betty moved her hand back to her tea cup. "Just because Trevor Stanton jumped into things that were not his business doesn't mean you need to let go of that lovely smile I've seen you wearing when a certain gentleman is in the room." Betty looked straight at her daughter, "You've just got to wrap your head around the idea that God may have bigger things in store for you than you previously thought. Faith is never a tiny step, honey; it has to be a violent jump in what seems like the wrong direction." She smiled and they heard a dish break and angry whispers being communicated by the children in the kitchen. The two women laughed as Eve started to get up, but her mother stopped her, "I'll get it, you take some time to pray and ponder, sweetie."

Eve found her way out to her father's workshop. Smiling softly to herself she enjoyed the sound of the hammer and the smell of fresh sawn wood. A pound went out of rhythm, followed by a thump and a curse that would have made most preachers blush. Eve found herself unable to stifle her laugh which bubbled out of her as she asked, "Are you okay?" Her father turned, with a surprised look, and his thumb in his mouth, when he stood up from retrieving his fallen hammer. "Yeah." he said as he pulled his thumb out to examine it. "I'll be just fine." he said, though Eve noticed he favored the injured digit as he positioned another board.

Eve took a moment to glance over what he was working on, "What are you making?" she asked. Lee didn't look up when he answered, "Oh…you know…just some crates, thought we might put some stuff in." Eve nodded and gave the matter little thought as she leaned against the doorpost and looked outside.

The yard glistened in the morning sun as the light was captured in the rain drops that were nestled in the new spring grass. Lee worked on fitting the boards together and asked, "How you doing Evie?" Eve sighed, how was she doing? She didn't know. All that she could seem to think about was an old but powerful dream she had had, many years before. She began to share the experience. "God showed me once, that I would have an opportunity, to climb up a mountain, I think it was a mountain of faith, and be with someone I loved, or chose to give into doubts and go back to where I had come from." Lee glanced up, "What did you do?" Eve sighed, "Well, in the dream, I went back. And when I woke up my heart was so broken. I felt as if I had lost everything I had ever hoped for. The dream always troubled me because I asked God to let me finish it, to go back and make a different choice, but I never have had another dream like that one." Lee lifted his pinky to get at an itch in his ear and asked, "Why do you think He never let you finish it?" Eve felt her heart all choked up inside, "Because, the dream allowed me to know the depth my fear could take me into disappointment." She paused and took a breath, "Also, I think maybe, the time of choice isn't to be had in the dream, but here and now." Eve had been facing out into the morning air and hadn't noticed that her father had set down his hammer and walked toward her. He wrapped an arm around her and she rested her head on his shoulder. Lee spoke, "Well, honey, 'faith is the substance of things hoped for, the evidence of things not seen.'" Eve knew that passage from the book of Hebrews well, yet the familiarity of the verse and beauty of the words didn't seem to do justice to the turbulent circumstances and violent emotions she was wading through in this living test that was proving her character as it brought her to her destiny. Lee spoke softly to his daughter, "If you truly believe something, you will walk toward it."

PART 12

For thus saith the Lord:
Like as I have brought all this
great evil upon this people,
So will I bring upon them the good
that I have promised them.(m)

Weary traveler, far from home,
Believe your heart will no longer roam.

Mr. Bates sat at Miss Ruth's kitchen table. His head was in his hands, in an attempt to curb the pounding that was being magnified by the bustle and noise of the other two boarders who were eating breakfast while with Miss Ruth. The two men were out the door and on with their day none too soon. Miss Ruth cleared Mr. Bates' plate and freshened up his tea before she decidedly sat down, as if prepared to devour him.

Mr. Bates tried to avoid eye contact. He could only guess what her comments would be on all that had transpired the night before.

Miss Ruth let out a low, "Hmmm." and continued to look him over closely, "How's your head feeling this morning? Did Mr. Stanton rattle anything loose?" Then she began to chuckle, softly at first but it grew steadily until she was rolling. Mr. Bates looked up at her, unsure of how to perceive her mood. Miss Ruth clapped her hands and caught her breath, "Lord Bless me. The image of Trevor Stanton's cigar being knocked right out of his mouth will surely warm my soul on cold dark nights for the rest of my days. Thank you Mr. Bates." she said and laughed again. Mr. Bates almost joined her, a sideways smile creeping up on his face, but the memories of his tussle with Stanton were framed with images of Eve, her face blank and shocked, soaking wet and shivering. What could she be thinking of him this morning?

He fostered some hope that Lee may soften Eve's heart to hear what he had to say, though he'd made Lee promise not to mention any of the details he had become privy to when they had that late night conversation. He knew Lee would keep his word on the matter.

Mr. Bates had become lost in his thoughts and looked up to Miss Ruth, who had stopped laughing and was again eyeing him carefully.

"Lord, Bless me child, you plum scared witless, Mr. Bates." Mr. Bates dropped his head and had to admit, "I had, before, very little hope that Eve would consider an offer from me, once my circumstances were made clear to her...now...I fear Stanton has done away with that."

Miss Ruth lifted a wrist to her hip and shook her head, "Poor man, you gotta rise up now. Rise up."

She sat thinking and then seemed to know how to proceed. "Mr. Bates, did I ever tell you how I got out West?" Mr. Bates shook his head, this turn in the conversation confusing him. "Well, my family was slaves, Mr. Bates. My granddaddy was granted his freedom, and daddy worked hard so that we could have a chance in this land. But back home, there wasn't much chance for black folk to make much of themselves. My mother took me aside that night my daddy died, and she gave me a box. This box was all the money they had saved my whole life. Mother sat me down and she spoke of learning to be a lamb, so we can grow into a lion." Mr. Bates was listening intently as Miss Ruth went on, "You see, she explained to me, that our people were made lambs, when they were forced into slavery. And, that it was a hard thing, but God allowed it, because He knew it was the only way our people would come in such great numbers to this land at that time. Because He knew this place needed a people who could show aspects of His character the way we could. God is three persons, Father, Son and Holy Spirit. Most people can't see it, Mr. Bates, but in every part of the world, God shows Himself through His children. Some people know about Jesus, some people understand the heart of the Father, and some people the Spirit. God brought all us people together in this land, just like an artist brings colors to a canvas, so He could paint a picture of Hisself for all the world to see. But we all gotta learn to rise up into that promise." Ruth's eyes glistened like deep pools. "Momma said, 'God done suffered us to be lambs so one day we could be lions.' Just like Jesus came as the Lamb and suffered to death, so that He could rise up and become the Lion." Miss Ruth grew thoughtful and saddened by distant memories, but she continued. "She gave me that box of money and told me to go, and I did. I took that hope they had saved away for me, and me and my husband decided to come out West, start a new life. He didn't make it. He died along the way, so I decided to come on alone. I couldn't manage our wagon myself, so I sold it and tried to buy passage on a stage, but a black woman wasn't allowed on a stage unless she was a slave or servant of a white passenger. So I paid one of the passengers to say I was his girl," she looked into Mr. Bates eyes, "I suffered being a lamb, being less than I was so that later I could rise up here and become a lion. I bought my own house and I run it my own way." Mr. Bates smiled at this truth he was now too familiar with.

Miss Ruth pointed at him, "Now, I'm telling you this story, because when I first saw you, I said, 'Lord, here comes one of your lambs, all tired and weary from his road' but I've seen you, I've been watching, and the Lord has blessed you in this place Mr. Bates. Your heart found rest from its wanderings and you done found love and joy. And now," she said and dropped her hands as if in defeat, "you gonna sit here, so beat up and tired that you're not willing to stand up and become a lion and fight for what is rightfully yours in the sight of God. So I'm gonna tell you, rise up and be a lion, John Bates! Take hold of God's blessings for your life, and don't let no one, not even your own doubts, pull them outta your hand."

Mr. Bates sat in stunned silence. He had never heard such a story that revealed so much of God's unseen intentions for mankind. Miss Ruth turned out of her chair and pointed to him as she moved on through the kitchen. "You done read her dreams didn't ya?" John looked up and nodded. Miss Ruth giggled, "The Lord is good. Now that taught you to hope didn't it?" Mr. Bates sighed, it had but the look on Eve's face haunted him. Miss Ruth sat down in front of him and waited till he looked her square in the eyes, "So the question is, are you gonna let something Trevor Stanton said in spite steal that hope, or are you gonna fight for it?"

"Now you think some on that, while you go get cleaned up, there ain't no way I'm letting you outta this house looking like something the cat dragged in. You have that town meeting at two; then you better get yourself all settled with that girl before you come home for supper tonight." And with that she flounced away and left Mr. Bates alone.

A test of faith, will long outlast,
the present, future, and the past
You didn't know all you could be,
at last His hand you now can see.

Eve deposited her father at the front of the meeting hall and took the team to the livery stable. The weather looked questionable, and with no knowing how long the meeting would be, Eve thought it best to house the horses and walk down town to visit Miss Ruth. There was so much she wanted to share with her, and yet at the same time, she didn't really want to talk about any of it. The truth was she simply wanted to spend some time in the company of her dear friend and let her heart rest from worry.

A crack of distant thunder caused Eve to look behind her at the storm clouds that were slowly but surely heading their way. Turning back she discovered that Trevor Stanton had emerged from the doorway of the meeting hall. He didn't notice her as he threw another cigar down and stomped it out. Eve didn't know if he had chosen to leave the meeting or been asked to leave. Either way didn't really matter. Eve actually felt a wave of pity wash over her. She didn't necessarily walk towards him; she simply didn't allow his presence to deter her from her path.

"How's it going in there?" she asked, trying to sound lighthearted and neighborly. Trevor turned and upon perceiving who had spoken, glared momentarily before looking away as if he hadn't heard her. Eve was undaunted, but feeling sad for his situation she went on, "I am very sorry for you Trevor, having so much of what you own suddenly devalued in such a way." She glanced out toward the mountains, not noticing the way he was already shaking his head, "but it's a big country, there are thousands of acres out there just waiting for you to claim." Trevor touched his brow lightly and turned toward her, "Well you see, Eve, that's just the problem. There are so many acres out there, so many valleys, how am I going to decide which one to pick? Do I choose this piece of land or that one? You seem to know how to choose one over the other, so why don't you tell me how it's done." He leveled his gaze and she knew full well his meaning. She knew her answer would sound simple and foolish, but it was still the truth, "God doesn't always give us the reasons why He has us go left instead of right." Trevor was shaking with emotion, "No, Eve, no, you can't blame God for your decision, even if you believe He inspired in one direction over the other, the choice was still yours." Eve pulled her wrap closer around herself. He was right and she could admit that. "Trevor, I simply never…I gave up my choosing a long time ago, when I put my trust in God." He looked up, "So what you're telling me is that you chose God, not him." Trevor pointed into the building he had just exited, motioning toward Mr. Bates. Eve felt suddenly ashamed of her feelings, but she dared to look Trevor Stanton in the eye when she said, "Sometimes, God's will is hard." Trevor glanced away; it was hard for him to meet her gaze. She had stood in her faith in the midst of her grief. He clucked his tongue and looked back, overcoming any pity he might have for her and he whispered with a sly smile and a nod toward the building where Mr. Bates was, "but not always." Eve glanced through the window at Mr. Bates and then back to Stanton, her lip trembled as she nodded and repeated his words, "No, not always." Trevor dipped his head so that the brim of his hat covered his face from her gaze. When he lifted it back up Eve was hit by the emotion displayed. He lifted two fingers and touching the brim of his hat he said with finality, "Well then, Mrs. Carson, I guess there's nothing more to say." And with that he strode off.

Hours later Eve walked through the town, the sunlight fading behind clouds once again. She'd had a pleasant visit with Miss Ruth. Eve always found peace in the walls of that house, despite the coming and going of boarders. The chill of coming rain caused her heart to cool another degree as well. Such a rainy spring could not be good news for the dam. She wondered how much time there really was left. How many people would truly move? How many would be willing to rebuild on higher ground without being able to gain anything by selling land or buildings that were in what was soon to be zoned, the floodway. Despite the tumultuous anxieties she was harboring about her more personal circumstances, she was eager to hear how the meeting had gone and what plans were being considered.

She hurried off toward the livery stable, as it was starting to rain and she was fairly sure she could find shelter there without having to deal with anybody.

The town meeting had adjourned, Lee and others began making small talk about the plans for Baker's Hill, one of the prime locations Mr. Bates had suggested as the new center of town. Mr. Bates had zoned areas, causing some relief as many realized that not all would be lost. A few main buildings such as the church were on the hill already on higher ground and could possibly survive the initial breach waters.

Mr. Bates felt a need for a break from such things and headed out, hoping for a leisurely walk back to Miss Ruth's, where Lee had informed him Eve most likely was. As he stepped out the door, he happened to see Eve going into the stable and feeling an urgency that surpassed his need for more preparation he followed after her.

Eve had just stepped up beside Lee's team of draft horses. A distant ray of sunlight invaded the dark storehouse. Straw dust appeared as leaves of gold floating in the air. Eve hardly noticed, she was tired and a bit wet. Her hand caressed one of the horses' long faces. Life, strong and vibrant snorted out of the nostrils at her touch. The horse bowed his face to hers and she lowered her forehead. She felt broken, like this horse, well tamed. No will of its own. No doubt he'd rather be in green fields, running into the wind that was bringing this new rain, but here he stood, patiently in a dark barn, his will bent to that of his master. Harnessed to a burden, partnered with another his master had chosen for him. Eve sighed, so God was with her. But she could feel herself, her own equine of will, raging against the coming of a new harness. Freedom had consoled her sorrow in a way and despite how much she missed the comfort of the guiding reins, part of her still despised them. Eve knew herself enough to recognize that nothing but the deepest of loves for her Master and for another such partner would induce her to take on that harness again. She was confused, she had thought…but she was human, she made mistakes. Silently she prayed that God would show her His way, yet again.

Mr. Bates entered, already dripping from the rain. "Eve." Her name came out like a statement, but when she turned toward him, she saw his eyes were searching, questioning. She took a deep breath and then a step toward him. He took a step toward her and pulled something out of the breast pocket of his jacket. Eve hoped that he hadn't written her a letter, which was what it appeared to be. Extending it toward her, the paper gently held so that his wet hand would do the least damage to it, he began to speak. "I hope you understand how desperately sorry I am for the way you learned of my plans." Eve nodded and blinked, the acknowledgement of the reality of his plans was causing her eyes to water. He was standing very close to her now and she became very aware of how near he was to touching her. The sound of the rain on the roof grew in intensity and Eve glanced up and saw the sun on the distant mountains, the light somehow traveling over the valley and through the rain. Golden, life giving rays rested, like a knowing hand, on Bates' shoulder, illuminating the white collar of his shirt. The light flickered into Eve's eyes and she was caught in a moment, in a memory. He wore no tie, his top button was open, the hollow where his collar bones met heaved slightly as he breathed. The angle of his chin line was outlined deeply in the light and shadows of the present sphere of time. Eve dared to look up at him, *him*, who seemed so close. Despite all her efforts to remain undisturbed by these revelations her heart warmed. Within her chest the essence of love, woman, wife awakened again simply by his presence.

The clouds moved as the wind shoved them aside and the light fell to the letter. Eve shook her head and glanced down.

She looked up and tried to stop herself from being swept away with the feelings that he provoked. "I understand, Mr. Bates…" but he interrupted her, "No you don't, I brought this so that you could." Eve looked down at the single sheet of paper, so small in comparison to what she had handed him, but all she could focus on were the last words he had spoken. Exhaling in acknowledgement of the fact that she was going to have to read a letter, right now, she took the paper and opened it.

Mr. Bates pivoted around her, remaining close but allowing the light from the open door to fall on the written words.

She read it through, at least twice, then glanced over certain bits yet again. Eve stood blinking at the letter. When she looked up her eyes were brimmed with tears that Mr. Bates understood. Eve choked back her emotions as she refolded the letter. She'd been so selfish! This man's family needed him and she had been trying to hold him here for herself. She felt completely ashamed and disappointed in herself. She hadn't, until now considered what his actual situation may be. "I'm sorry Mr. Ba…"shaking her head she resorted to a simpler path, "John, I didn't know…or, I mean I guess I…but, it's alright," she looked into his face. "Your family needs you at home…I can't expect you to stay and sort out our problems…" she pushed the paper into his chest and brushing passed him, she walked out the door. The words seemed etched into her mind, words that bore into her soul, awakening the Maker's preparations in her heart yet again. Still, the reality was overwhelming and Eve, in shock, chose to disbelieve that she had known. She was overcome by the realization that Mr. Bates had a life and home she had not considered. Others who loved and needed him. She felt so foolish! Of course he had other obligations than just making her dreams come true.

Mr. Bates followed her and catching up to her he grabbed her gently by the shoulders and made her look at him and gave her a little shake, "Eve, I'm not saying good-bye!" His hands felt like heavy weights on her shoulders, Eve tried to brush them off, but they didn't move. He knew this was his last chance and he suddenly found a lion waking up deep within him. He wasn't going to let go. He took a breath and lowered his tone, "I want to know if you will come with me. Eve, for now, and trust we will end up where we belong." he said in a much softer tone, "Will you marry me?"

Eve lifted her eyes to his, but it was another voice that rose in answer to John's question.

"Well there we have it, ladies and gentlemen!" Trevor Stanton stood at the end of the porch in front of the General Store, a gun in one hand and a half empty bottle of whiskey in the other. Mr. Bates moved as if to pull Eve behind him, but Stanton continued, "Hey, hey, don't do that!" he smiled coyly as he cocked his pistol, "cause I haven't decided which one of you I'm going to shoot first." Mr. Bates stopped moving and Eve tried to remember to breathe. She hadn't thought Trevor capable of this. Stanton went on, in an uninhibited manner that testified of his bottle of half- drunk courage. "Should I shoot the woman I love, because she refuses to love me back, or should I shoot the man who has taken everything, and I mean everything that I hold dear? My good name, my town, my…" he stopped and looked at Eve, "well I guess she never was mine, but hey, I was at least in the running before you showed up." Stanton laughed at himself and then grew somber, "I could do anything, I have everything, except hold back one little river. Years of work, of accumulating wealth and for what? It's all deemed worthless." and he lifted the bottle in a salute to this fact and took a sip. His eyes dropped and Eve dared to hope that he wouldn't actually shoot anyone, when out of nowhere it seemed, a frying pan lifted up and knocked Stanton in the back of the head. The impact threw his body forward and his gun went off. Eve caught a glimpse of Miss Ruth as Stanton fell but her senses were overpowered by other sensations as power deep and penetrating knocked her off her feet. She tried to focus and make sense of what she was feeling and seeing but she could not. It was as if she was swallowed up into a great blue cloud.

Lightening crashed filling the clouds with bolts of fire. The dark blue shrouds glowed with the flashes as a veil before a flame. Far below the storm the rain landed upon the waves of the lake each drop adding to the pressure. Finally, the weight reached the breaking limits of the dam. The stone giant was torn apart by the raging river.

The sunlight of a new day glistened upon the water as it tore its way with white capped claws and a foaming mouth through the valley below. Nothing escaped its carnivorous appetite as it devoured the town of old Frontier. Eve was aware that all of this was happening but she was outside of time and in another place.

In the cloud Eve was not alone, a presence, very old and full of love and light was beside her. She knew Him and His name but she afterward always referred to Him as the Ancient One. His voice filled the cloud. It was the sound of the rain and of the lightning bolt and the clap of the thunder. Eve was shaking her head. He was the only thing that wasn't moving within the swirling blue floating depth.

"Please look." He said and Eve turned her gaze as He parted a tiny portion of the cloud where she saw a tumult of bodies erupt out of the opening and charge past her. She saw a battle. Gruesome beasts ravaged and struck at people who looked like her, who were fighting back. She knew she had been fighting as well. Then the sound of hoof beats overtook the snarling gnashing sounds of fangs and swords and a magnificent Centaur, like blue flame proceeded through the opening. He held a bow and arrows and ran stomping out the images of the lower beasts. The Centaur ran straight over Eve knocking her back while everything went into a bright light. Then very normal rustic scenes began to play as if a dream before Eve's eyes.

She saw Josiah's accident, and she saw the Ancient One take his heart out of the body afterward.

Eve was surrounded in peace and lay in a strange place. Fog was all around. She was reaching trying to get to that 'other' place where Josiah was, but he was too far away.

Above her stretched out a huge talon of an eagle which raked across her chest, tearing her heart out as well.

Eve lay still and looked as the claw hung over her, a piece of her torn heart still hanging from its sharp end. Eve lifted her hand and able to reach it, she took hold of the piece of her heart and pulled it back. That was when she saw that it was not a torn piece, but a new young heart, although she was deeply aware that for a short time her chest had been empty.

Eve looked up and witnessed many things. She saw the details of Josiah's death, the tumbling of rocks and rushing of water. Eve saw something she had never known before. Josiah had told a man about the Lord through his death. Eve saw that the man was changed by what occurred. She was filled with love, a holy love for mankind, each individual and how even a death could be used to show someone a glimpse of the Creator.

The Ancient One came near to Eve, tears were rolling out of the corners of her eyes as she looked up at Him. With a fatherly expression He took the new small heart and placed it back in her chest. Light came from His hand which closed the wound, leaving a scar that shimmered like pearl. He healed only a large part of the tear, there was a small portion that would have to heal in time. He smiled down, all luminous and loving and Eve smiled back for she was allowed to see His hurt and how He had overcome the loss of His heart once and the pains and travails He had endured to get it back.

He sat down beside her. Eve's chest ached badly, but He looked proudly upon her. "The world is lost, Eve. It is a dark and cruel place, but it does not have to be all that men know. They can know this place, they can know Me, but few seek to." This saddened Him, "It is because there is a cost, as you know. It is painful to suffer. But it is not needlessly done. I have my reasons." He looked at her and lowered His face, "I am sorry that your path was so hard for you, but you needed the promise and his love beforehand to get you through. Many must be made to go back, but you have chosen to, because of your love for him, and that was my plan." He smiled. Eve noticed his beard and the brightness of the place made His face hard to see. It was more that she could feel His smile than see it. He reached and placed a hand over her head and Eve felt the physical world pulling her back. It was in pain that she came to her senses.

Her shoulder ached and she gasped as she opened her eyes to daylight. The brightness faded quickly as her eyes adjusted. She was in a room in a bed of white, though she was still aware of where she had been only a moment ago. Laying her head back she thanked God that she was alive. Her movements were noticed by someone sitting beside the bed and a hand, large and warm seemed to swallow hers up. Looking over she saw her dad. His face was ravaged with concern and he looked as if he hadn't slept for days. She said his name softly, questioningly and relief poured out of him and threatened to become laughter. "Thank God you're alright. You lost so much blood the doctor didn't know if you were going to pull through." Eve realized something more had happened to her than what she had known on the other side. "Did Trevor shoot me?" Lee shook his head, "Well, he didn't mean to, the gun went off when someone hit him from behind." Eve smiled, "Miss Ruth tried to help."

Eve stared up at the ceiling in wonder. It felt strange, like waking from her dreams often did. She seemed to come to a point of understanding and focus and turned her face to her father, "The kids, are they alright?" Lee nodded, "I'd better go tell them you're awake and get the doctor." Eve watched him walk around the foot of the bed, "Dad," she said and he stopped and rested his hand on the frame his eyes eager for what she may need, "is John still here?" Lee's face erupted in a huge smile, "I wondered how long you'd let that sit, do you want to see him?" Eve felt weak but nodded and Lee turned chuckling to himself. She must be feeling better!

Her mother, kids, and Miss Ruth and so many others wanted to see her, mostly to calm their own anxieties. Eve took it as an expression of love. She was relieved to see her children. They were a soothing balm to her wounded soul, although their antics and hugs caused her shoulder to begin to ache. The doctor was concerned for her and chased out the visitors so he could examine her. When he came out of the room, Mr. Bates had arrived with Blue Cloud. They stood in the hall and listened to the doctor as he spoke to Lee. The doctor's eyes looked out from under his bushy brows and over the rims of his glasses. "It's a bad wound, but she's strong. My real concern is the loss she's recently been through. Emotional pain like that can cause some to lose heart, to lose the will to fight and live…that's what she needs right now."

John Bates timidly entered the room and saw that Eve was awake, though pale. The doctor watched him go with interest. A knowing look from Blue Cloud confirmed his hope and he smiled and turned away no longer worried about Eve's will to go on.

Eve smiled at John and he walked in silence across the floor and sat down in the chair next to her bed. Emotions welled up in her, more than she could contain and despite her efforts to control them, tears splashed out of her eyes. John leaned forward in concern, "Take it easy, it's alright." Eve nodded and took a deep breath. "I want to tell you…how very sorry I am." John lowered his head and dared to reach out and touch her hand. Looking up he spoke, "I know…it's alright." Eve saw what he was thinking and took a firm hold of his hand and shook it, "No John, I'm sorry that I didn't know, I didn't think I was ready to meet you. I'm sorry for how much I've been wrestling against my own heart. He made me ready for you, but I fought him. I thought it was wrong, I thought I needed time to make it feel proper. But now I know His will is proper, no matter what it seems like to us." Laying her head back she closed her eyes as her recent encounter flooded her mind.

Her eyes were opened up toward the ceiling as she spoke. "I saw God." She said. "Josiah was with him." Eve said it so simply, with perfect peace and not overwhelming emotion, that John sat stunned. A type of strange reserve settled on him as he realized that he sat next to a person who had drawn near to the borderlands that separate the realms of God and man. "God told me…He told me…" Eve was finding it hard to put the experience into words, and the things God had said now didn't seem like words at all but a type of knowing and she couldn't seem to express. Her face became a picture of frustration and John spoke, "Just rest now, Eve." Eve didn't listen, "No, there's something…I have to…" and Eve looked at John. She knew he needed to understand. She so desperately wanted to tell him. And then, suddenly it all fell into place and she knew all she needed to say. "I have to say, yes." Eve held his hand and looked to his face for understanding and repeated, "Yes.", but he was puzzled and responded, "Yes, you have to say yes?" Eve smiled, this was her moment, the moment of choosing and as she did a wall of rock that was nestled in the hills, lots its grip on the river it had been holding back, and a gushing flow of untamable wildness rushed through Frontier, taking away the old and releasing the violent hope of a 'new' Frontier. It may seem strange to some to think it a good thing when the crushing water ravaged the small town, its white rapids appearing like jagged teeth as it tore through the buildings, taking with it those who hadn't moved to higher ground. It was a horrible happening that had to come, just like Josiah had to leave. Because nothing on this Earth lasts forever, only God's love remains, and as He saw fit to build the dam, He knew the time of its collapse. He also was the author of the new set of plans for the town, and not the town only but the Native Village and the mining camp, for the failing of the dam brought them all together in a new way. Still all of this was just being born as Eve lay in bed, wounded, but in love. "I came back, to say yes to you." Then it was as if that light, that light from the other place filled John's eyes and he bowed his head as a feeling of intense gratitude overwhelmed him. It had been an incredible night for him, to come to realize that he had wanted to share his life with her, only to see her snatched away and to have to face the possibility that he would lose what he had hoped to gain.

There is much that could be told about the things that happened next, about the wedding, and the journey they embarked on together. But I will say only this, everything that God said would happen to Eve, did happen, the good and the bad. In the end the good was so very good that it overwhelmed all the pain and Eve forgot her sorrow, just like the river breached the dam that had held it back. She was able to thank God for the strange way He had brought her the strength she needed to live on; which is precisely what she did.

AFTERWARD

They that sow in tears shall reap in joy.
He that goeth forth and weepeth,
bearing precious seed,
Shall doubtless come again with rejoicing,
bringing his sheaves with him.(n)

A mother feels a burden heavy,
when chicks are young and days are cold
But a breath of heaven blows so sweetly,
when dreams, remembered, are retold.

Eve stepped out of the boys' room and made her way down the hall to tuck Julie in. Her heart felt heavy, but she thought it was only because she was so physically tired. She was on the mend, plans were being made and today had been the day when she had spoken to her children about moving, very far from the only home they had ever known.

Hearing a sound she glanced out the window at the end of the hall and saw her father loading the trunks he had made, but she had filled, into the back of the wagon. She smiled at the way he had apparently so easily heard and obeyed God on the matter.

Julie called out for her and Eve stood and moved on giving a reassuring, "I'm coming." Turning the corner into the doorway she saw Julie, small for her twelve years, sitting in bed haloed by the low glow of her lamp. Eve entered, sat on the edge of the bed and hugged her. Julie lay back and snuggled into her covers and looked up at her mother. Julie had been thinking. Eve smiled down at her, "Are you alright, sweetie?" Julie did a slight shrug and glanced away and Eve could see she was trying not to cry. She covered her daughters hands with her own, "Oh, honey, tell me what's wrong." Eve knew it could be anything, from leaving her grandma and papa so quickly to a fear of sharks as they would be crossing an ocean soon.

Julie looked at her hands and began, "Momma, I remembered something today, when you were talking about going on the boat to get to England." She sighed and shifted around in her covers. Eve brushed her hair off of her forehead, "What's that?"

Julie took a breath and went on, emotion cracking her voice at times, "I remembered, when I was little, before Daddy died, I had dreams of a ship. I dreamt of Daddy having to go away on a ship across a sea to a place I couldn't go and I would get scared and cry." Eve stroked her hair, "Yes, honey I remember when you had those dreams." Julie, sighed and was almost lost in her emotion but managed to speak, "Well, I didn't know what it meant then, just that I wanted my daddy and I couldn't go with him, but now…I know, I understand it was about him having to die, wasn't it mommy?" Eve had tears running silently down her face as she answered, "Yes, honey, it was. It was God's way of telling your heart what was going to happen." Julie had to manage her breathing, but seemed able to do it well, as if the hard part of what she wanted to say was over.

She looked out the window of her room again and then, asked, "Mommy, you had dreams like that too, didn't you?" Julie looked at her hands, not wanting to see her mother's face if the question didn't set well. Eve nodded, "Yes, baby, I had dreams like that too, but…at first I didn't want to understand what God was saying, and I remember when you had your dreams because they taught me to trust God, even when I didn't want to. When you told me those dreams, it was like I could see that this was bigger than just me, and my sadness.

We were all going to have sadness, but God was talking to you too and watching over all of us and I trusted that He would always do that, no matter what happened."

Julie smiled, a tender loving smile at her mother and tilting her head she continued, "At first, when I remembered the dreams, I was angry, because they had been so scary to me, but now I think that God didn't want me to be scared, even though He probably knew I would be. But He went ahead and gave me that dream anyway, because He knew we'd be here today, and I think He wanted us to be happy for Daddy, cause Daddy's with God, and they're happy together."

Eve was nodding and had to struggle to say, "I think you're right honey."

Julie reached up and gently touched one of her mother's tears, and spoke "So sometimes, we may miss Daddy, but we don't have to cry anymore. You know why?"

Eve looked at her questioningly, "Why?"

Julie answered, "Because, just like we can be happy that God and Daddy are together, I think they are happy that now we are going to be together, with Mr. Bates, going on our ship to our new place."

Eve scooped her daughter up and almost crushed her in an embrace. "I think you're right, sweetie."

Eve's heart was heavy, sadness and love mingled together so sweetly she could barely hold herself together as she walked silently into her own little room and closed the door.

She fell to her knees, letting her bed catch her by her arms and through the overwhelming waves of emotion she thanked God for life, bittersweet as it was and worth every tear.

Scripture References.
  *New Kings James

a. Song of Solomon 5:2
b. Daniel 4:5
c. John 3:7
d. John 13:19
e. Psalm 71:20
f. John 1:6
g. Isaiah 42:9
h. Jeremiah 10:19
i. Romans 4:17
j. Psalm 105:19
k. Isaiah 57:1
l. Hebrews 10:9
m. Jeremiah 32:42
n. Psalm 126:5,6

About the Author

JESSICA HECKET was born in Coeur d'Alene, Idaho, and has grown up in the surrounding areas. She met God when she was seven years old and has loved him ever since. She is now a wife and mother whose art and dreams are often inspired by God and infused with her love of nature and horses.